Published by IPBo

© IPBooks 2021
(Seventh edition ISB

All rights reserved. V   under
copyright reserved ab   part of this publication may be reproduced, stored or introduced into a retrieval system, or transmitted, in any form or by any means (electronic, mechanical, photocopying, recording or otherwise), without the prior written permission of both the copyright owner and the publisher of this book.

A CIP catalogue record for this book is available from the British Library.

1

I was right about the floods. A parent's evening thwarted progress for a second week. By the good grace of God, she arrived after three weeks of displeasure, albeit slightly late. Ecstatic and full of resolve was I.

Pre-planning was to be put to good use and by the skin of my teeth I managed to pull it off. I asked her if she would help me with this new move that I had devised. Laura's move. That is what it will be called, and it was only devised because of her. I had sketched it out whilst listening to my favourite music at high volume. A little later I realised that I could double its length by running it out again. This time in reverse with her in front of me instead. Then came that light bulb moment of fantasy. Both men and women can lead in the same dance. This move hands the lead over.

A few women have been doing the leading for a while and the concept has fair appeal. Some will think it is stupid. Some will see it as way too complicated, but some will treasure it for sure. It will please some, not all, but please this smallish group a lot. I state to myself that I shall only dance this move, this first stab at a move that has this lead/follow switch with Laura and Laura only. We shall perform it and wait for someone to pick up on it. A lot of work is needed though as I want to add flourishes with the spare arms and include head flicks etc. There will be a different dance jig each time according to the mood and flavour of the music.

There are some four maybe five songs in the lesson interval. I get asked to dance by two people. The second was on autopilot as I am trying to position myself ready to ask Laura up. She has had a dance with what appears to be a full-of-himself office salesman. He is now talking with her about something or other. For ages. Then he gestures to her for another dance. Not a chance mate. It is all so disturbing for me. She says his name and "maybe in a bit", as I snatch the opportunity with microseconds to spare. She seems to know him more than me and I can't recall seeing him before. He is probably a fine fellow. Whatever the case, you are not getting two dances, not with Laura, not tonight.

I know from experience that when I try showing her the move there will be a point of 'shall we leave it there'. When it doesn't go quite to plan, peak discomfort rears up. The temptation to quit, stop, and sit down beckons. I was not wrong. I was however, determined that I will not put a halt to it until enough had been laid down. We will carry on regardless. The fun that is to be had messing about with someone so piquant is remarkable. It is a long-complicated move but to be fair the only tense part was getting her turning in the right direction. She must keep her feet in the same spot, so they wrap over when turning around under her arm.

I realise later that having your arm bent back over your shoulder, whilst holding each other's hands, leads to a lowered neck position. Not super comfortable. A bend in the knees whilst leaning back a little solves this. Something to show her next week. Anyway, we did a few run throughs, and I am happy. Very. A short set of familiar moves later and I reiterated the purpose. This is for the women. I have done it. I got in, in the nick of time. I saw her again. I danced with her again and having sat with her for a few minutes she joined the lines – in front of me. A first. Let me explain.

(People form lines with the women standing in front of the men. The teacher will get everyone to do a bit then the women move along one and repeat the section with the next person in the line.)

A few weeks prior I was at my most inept. I had asked her about a dance weekend, and it was a bit confuddled. I left her to it for a short while and then headed in her direction hoping to start the session with her. I gave her two thumbs up at waist level and she did the same. She did not stand in front of me though. She waited and mumbled something about wanting to see what is happening. Then she joined some way away. Not good. It means I may only get her visiting me once rather than twice. I know. Women have told me they align themselves in such a fashion to avoid certain people. Some are heavy-handed. Some are rough. Some are both rough and critical. They will tell the women off, not in a nice way either. They start on the left of the person they are trying to avoid so that, at worst, they only have to dance with them once, sometimes not at all if there are lots of people there. It can take a good fifteen minutes to get around, dancing a little bit with each person in turn. If Laura is selecting a start point unfavourable to me, it is a set back at the very least. People say that I am a smooth dancer, and I never tell anyone off no matter how badly they mess up. I haven't forgotten what it was like to be a beginner. I want to encourage people to keep coming, not put them off.

A reader will soon gather that Laura is not heading in my direction at all. I am not stupid. The idea of us being an 'us' is truly bonkers. It is not really what it is about. There is no need to sneer. I have flash feelings of worthlessness from time to time, but I have had more than enough opportunities. Some I missed and some I took up. Laura doesn't look at me. Laura does not smile at me. I know this. I also know she has never come over to me, not once. She is just making me feel irrelevant. I am not complaining, I too have ignored others in the same way.

I am familiar with those that played chess by post. They would write down their move on a postcard and it would get sent back and forth. The match would drag on for months. Some make it even more sublime by sending the move once a year at Christmas. This game of Laura is slow and shite too. With a crap ending most likely. I say shite, what I mean is the drudgery of seven days, seven nights until the next encounter. My productivity has hit the lowest level ever seen in my life. I go play some sports. I do an hour of work at the computer trying over and over to appease endless customers. Every day it is the same. Where is my item? What is the tracking number? People pay next to nothing for an item and assume that it will be delivered via limousine by an awakened Santa Claus, hours after they pressed buy it now. Still, I earn plenty from it. Maybe writing about the pathetic details of dallying with Laura will assist in the catharsis, the acceptance, the pretence, the sorrow, and injustice of it all.

I intend to sow a seed. I will weave an image of fantasticalness in relation to sailing. I might ask her directly whether she will accompany me on a trip to Greece, on a most excellent boat. Beautiful bays for lunch, dolphins riding the bow and places to dance most evenings. If I look at this proposition from her point of view, it is clear that whilst a nice idea, it is not sufficiently inviting. She doesn't know me well enough. She might like to go, maybe, just not with me. No serious chance of that. Not at this point anyway. Seeds do linger. A seed could help further down the line. I need to find other enticements too. Plant, plant, plant and maybe the slowly slowly catchy monkey might bear fruit.

Another plan is forming too. I wear a hat. It is essential to hold it firmly when ducking under her arm at the beginning of Laura's move. Thankfully, I tested this bit out with someone else beforehand. The hat came off.

Not good. She mentioned that maybe she might need a hat too. Thus, I have bought a nice feminine silver-grey cap-hat. This will go on her head right away next week. I'll ask if she is going to the dance night on Saturday and if she wants to visit a rather good Indian restaurant nearby first. The restaurant is very good, that I know for sure. So, what do I anticipate? I expect a no. Whatever the response, I will say little and appear amused, not upset. I want to leave myself in the position to be able to ask again. If I can't persuade her then I will give her a copy of my book as a last roll of the dice measure.

A sprightly twenty-two-year-old named Megan has entered the dance scene. Although half my age, she is twice as decent. She appears to be somewhat true to herself. In that I mean her presentation is not in accordance with the latest guidance on 'social' media. Very short hair, shaved like it would be on the first day as an army recruit. A genuine woman with unshaved legs, hairy armpits and a smile that beams welcome. As one who advocates finding the courage to be true to oneself, I can only look on in sheer admiration. I have a ploy to infuse myself into people's consciousness; Having seen her with a distinctly crumpled grey dress thing on, I kindly remark that "I see you have been given an iron for Christmas". On another occasion I push the boundaries of indecency. "Have you been doing it doggy style this week?" A long stare. A long pause. Then a laugh of sorts after I remind her "You are a dog groomer are you not?" I have many rules. One joke loaded with inuendo is semi-acceptable. Once. I will not make two jokes like this as that is not funny anymore. Three and it is sexual harassment.

I can get away with a little as I have had some discussions with her a few times. Outside cooling off, dancing is heat inducing, I utilised some complex jargonistic words during a three-way exchange. Megan, myself, and an elderly gentleman. Megan had not heard these terms before. I said to her, "I'll buy you a dictionary. Seeing as you are a vegetarian you can eat it and absorb all the words." She said that I was a 'mad hat philosopher' which unbeknownst to her, is a handle I had recently used on a video channel. Megan stands in stark contrast to Laura. Nevertheless, anyone lucky enough to be a bedfellow with her will not encounter the illness of self-centeredness. She talks and listens. She takes on board what you are saying. Laura does too. Laura may ignore me in many respects, but she has engaged in fantastic conversations with me.

Megan wants to learn the lead. I want to have a bash at following. I will need it soon. I believe Laura mentioned she wants to learn the lead as well. Learning to lead with someone that is inexperienced with following is mighty tough. It is much easier with someone that can follow already, IE another woman. We have a go. Tonight, is not our first attempt. The "let's leave it there" pops up, but she is more comfortable, not really giving a damn, and just keeps attacking it. I lead the move quickly first, to work out which arm goes where. Then let Megan try. I have to learn dancing from another angle too. I need to step back with the other leg. I must respond to the turns, in the right direction.

This was a good session, a really good one. All the chairs have been stacked away and we are virtually the only ones left. Absorbed in what we are doing. Unfortunately, I have an image of Laura walking past us on the way out. She did say goodbye, albeit in a nonchalant fashion. She was like a vanguard ship heading straight out, not wavering her eyes in our direction. I know all people are equally valid. I know Megan is someone that is evolving into a real dance mate. However, the distinction between Laura and Megan is phenomenal. What I would do to swap these over. Have Laura doing this with me instead of Megan. Jolly mean really, as Megan always smiles at me, always looks at me and treats me with goodness.

I do recall having a go at following some years back. This lady had a big frame and a cherub face. She had said weeks before that "I'm not feeling it", when I was leading. These are just the comments one needs to keep your confidence running high. Tonight, it all changed between us with her leading me. It was a bit of a turnaround. It was amusing and enjoyable. She had the patience to give me a chance and we got on great doing this.

As for feeling it. Half-way through a dance I really felt it. Hard to explain and put into words, but jolly pleasant experience. It was with someone that I had never danced with before. A kind of dance orgasm that came about. I have no idea how to induce or replicate it. A sensation of paradise, lost in what we were doing, and caught up in it for a minute or so.

The dichotomy burns. On the one hand it is impossible. On the other it just might happen. The plan needs refinement. I have the most tenuous grip with panic and hysteria setting in across the globe. Will the UK shutdown? Will there be a momentous, destructive gap in the dance diary? Dancing could cease for weeks, potentially. The floods stole at least one evening already. If she does come next week then I must push. I predict a rejection. Laura is level 10. She has plenty of experience in this matter. I know she must have battered off endless, countless, relentless requests for more. She will be pleasantly unaccommodating and the urge to leave her alone will be strong.

I can use some Hocus Pocus palmistry. I have after all, used the 'lazy octopus' move many times with her that gave me a good look at the lines on her hand. I can tell her that one path is more vivid than the other. Life for you is going to be good regardless, but there is a choice. You have made many good choices so far. This choice is potentially intense and more notable. I only want a night out anyway. Will the hat sway anything? Will she accept it. Will she keep it on for any length of time? It doesn't matter. You can dwell on silly details.

A different spot tonight gives me a better view of everyone there and I eye the door for her late arrival. It looks like I will only get one mini-dance with Laura in the first half. I should have stood to the left of Denver. Denver is an eager dancer, a bit of a case, faux shy, a likable sort. He has gone from zero to five nights a week dancing in a short space of time, to become a super enthusiast. A lot of miles travelled. "I get to tangle with hundreds of women. Who gets to do that?", is his catch line.

I congratulate, I smile, I radiate some nervousness and point out that she did well with the new move inaugurated last week. I give Laura the hat and she put it on, takes it off, puts it back on at an angle then suggests that it is best to be worn for the new move. It is all good. She is not really a hat person and there is no disquiet from me. The focus is on asking her out. Directly. These moments are so ridiculously short. I am only any good with lengthy engagements.

We had a second go at Laura's move. I was about to suggest that it would be an idea to lean back when the arm is behind her head. Before I opened my mouth, she made that exact suggestion. This is great. She got it. She is on it. I am pleased by this. I have someone now. Someone that is perfect for moving my kind of dancing onwards and upwards.

The sense of purpose is there for sure. I will sit next to her regardless, no fussing, no dilly dallying. I have a new red hat and she asks me why. I tell her that the other one has worn out. It is a truth of sorts. The heat plays havoc with the longevity and might be undesirably noticed given that people connect in close quarters. I will tell you about small things. The first one; she never has any qualms about me or anyone taking a seat next to her. Some will shift a bit in their seat. Not Laura, that is a small thing that I appreciate.

In my youth, I recall a live eel that was kept fresh in a light blue bucket at a friend's house. Only those that have tried will know that trying to pick one up is decidedly difficult. Laura is a slippery eel. I mention the restaurant. Her face lights up and she nods vigorously agreeing how good it is. "How about dinner and dance on Saturday?", I ask. This rapidly changes her facial expression. First to shock followed by mild nausea - horrified. Her face is hilarious. She speaks volumes through it, telling me the truth. She is not terribly keen on that town for some reason. I know she has been to a dance there before though. It might be misdirection. The town in question has probably got nothing to do with it.

She tells me about the swimming gala at her school and I enquire as to whether she is a good swimmer or not. That may play when I one day ask her to join me on a sailing trip. I ask her what she is going to be doing instead on Saturday. There is a mention of going climbing. I establish where, though for some reason, even though she tells me twice it is a name that won't stick in my head. It is in a mountain range – not too far away. I envisage climbing gear and ropes etc, but no, it is a two-hour doable hike. I asked her if I could come too. But she is not sure if it will be this week. It all depends on the weather. "We don't want to get lost." The temptation is there to say, "I thought this was what you are doing on Saturday", but resist as I adopt the 'no arguing in dating' rule.

I do honestly like hikes of this nature. A hike with Laura would be just the ticket – many hours to elicit what I need plus any time with her is a monumental pleasure. The last mini mountain I ascended was in Curacao. It had a bit of a scramble and squeeze through large rocks at the summit. Do I give up and hand over the book? It is a decision that has pressure attached. It could ruin it all. The plague is getting serious. This may be the last time I have the indulgence of her company for a while. With resignation and sadness, I decide there is no other choice. My tear ducts should be running dry, they are not. Small bursts of weepiness. Pathetic but uncontrollable.

I have established one thing for sure. Laura is a jolly happy person. Perpetual joviality.

Looking back, I realise that the virus had come to town already. The head fog, the weepiness is reported by others too that caught it. I had had a mighty odd week of coughing like crazy. Just as you are about to drift off to sleep. I also felt unbelievably cold for a couple of days. Cold even in front of the wood burner. No major deal, nothing like other bugs I had. Just a little different. Steve had it a little worse than me. He spent sixty-three days on a ventilator before appearing back on the circuit right as rain later in the year.

I ask myself "what would I be doing, were Laura not about to toy with?" The melancholy is not entrenched. It is floating in and out. Things are good. Health is good. This Laura project is all consuming though. No other project is worthy of such attention. The writing is only Laura based. The thoughts and objectives are all Laura based too. This is a fine experiment that is giving me ideas. People give me ideas from time to time. Two ideas from the same person is rare. In this case Laura has given me five. This is a valuable process. I know the idea of us getting together is absurd. I write as such in the Laura section. It is an exploration, a chance to test things and an opportunity to put theories into practice.

There were many odd coincidences. I was in the process of editing and adding a few lines to the section about relationships and dating. I pulled the lines apart. Changed a few bits about then thought, hold on .... Laura! How about a first-person account of the interactions? A week of cobbling it together and I have ordered a proof copy of the next edition that I can give to her for approval. The inner/exterior beauty facet of life, interests me. I make, what I see, as a minor revelation. The inner and outer are connected. I test the theory out on a bunch of other philosophers, and it has legs. Laura decides what makeup to wear, what clothes to put on, how to have her hair etc. Those ideas come from within. Our personality inside us, reflects how we look on the outside. There is a lot more to it that, that I won't go into here.

Aside from the numerous problems, facts and issues that hold me and Laura at a distance, there is a lack of sleep problem that is a nuisance. I am not sure if the head fog stems from the lack of sleep or from the virus. Whatever the cause, it makes talking and dancing much harder. The mistakes I make with everyone, Laura included with the move we are learning tonight are clear to see. She even sighed a "oooh-aww", when I didn't do what I can usually do with ease. I am there but not there. I am using the limited resources I have, to decide what to say, what to ask and how to press home an intention. Sorry everyone. I only have time for Laura this evening. I won't let this slip for it is just too significant.

There is frustration and a small amount of exasperation pervading my thoughts. This is linked to a hideous amplification of the desire to befriend Laura. There is no time to experiment with hocus pocus. There is no time to mention destiny. There is just another week of solemnity looming.

You can't buy love. You can't invoke magic. You can't alter the unalterable.

I wait by the exit, no interest or energy or will or anything for anyone else there. She tends to have just one dance at the end before grabbing her stuff and leaving. A predictable routine. She walks towards me and stops, handing me the hat back. The hat is of little interest to me. It is an irrelevant gimmick that was unlikely to yield anything anyway. Maturity lends a hand in knowing what is best to do. We walk out the door together and once around the corner I announce that this is her contribution to philosophy.

"Philosophy", she says in a semi-surprised, vaguely impressed fashion. I point out that there are a couple of pages that she may be interested in. She says, "see you next week", in a warm friend to friend manner. I really do hope so.

My paranoia and assume-the-worst feelings are that she may chuck it, not pay any attention to it or in some way or another, disregard it. Will she read it and say nothing, then slip up by saying something that alludes to having read it? I don't expect any concern. I am sure that it will be radio silence until next week.

I will fill this week by filling you in about other fine people that gyrate to the hall each week. Beforehand I need to decide if I will also use what I know to rectify the Laura on my mind all the time misadventure. One visualisation trick used a few times will make Laura drop out and disappear forever. I will soon forget that I forgot all about her.

Maybe I should have been more patient. Maybe some patience and persistence could at the very least lead to a good friendship. Firstly, you have to be in it to win it. Secondly it would be comical if someone found this tale of haplessness entertaining.

We think about us, we, me, I. We think about ourselves. I am looking at this far too much from my perspective. She cares a little, she cares a little for all the dancers there. She doesn't care for me markedly more than anyone else. Each paragraph in the tiddly piece 'Laura' in the book has potential errors and potential missights. I may have got a lot wrong. It could all be wide of the mark entirely. Whatever the case, it does suggest that I have a crush on her. That might not be a positive from her vantage point. I have elevated Laura in a book where I enjoy nothing more than de-elevating people. Sometimes in a cynical way. It can recalibrate the lives of those that think they are great, bringing them down to earth.

Who else is notable? We have a pair of Michelle's. They car share. One is a time-warped nineteen-fifties' wonder lady. An artist, sculptor who dances with zest. She has a jig that differs from most. A lucky husband doesn't attend. The other is a teacher's sidekick – a follower for the demonstrator. She sounds like she knows a thing or two about garden maintenance. As for dancing, one of the best. I can spin her fast, move her in any direction that I want, as I want, and expect.

I have absolutely no idea what move we are supposed to be doing as I am talking with Michelle rather than paying attention. She asks, do you know what to do? Nope, not a clue. This arouses laughter time after time. If I get a brief look at the teacher, I can enact what is needed. If I have not seen a thing, then I just watch the people on my right and I am soon up to speed. Alternatively, I just do it all wrong and not care one jot. She kicked me a few weeks back. "Wake up, get with it." I am glum. I am sure you can work out the reason. I do get into the groove though, irrespective of who is there or not. It is hard to hide one's feelings, I am in the pub and a friend is asking me why I was in a bad mood, "coming on strong last Tuesday". He said another friend had noticed too. Monday was not what I was hoping for.

A birthday custom: A large circle forms around the one-year-older person. After a few solo jigs they pull a few quick moves with a wide selection of those in the surrounding group. On Michelle's birthday she made a bee line for me, for me first. I will own up to something. I have on a couple of occasions got closer than what is deemed necessary with Michelle. I avoid getting carried away on the whole, but on some nights, it is potentially convivial. I will only admit doing the same with one other person. Not Laura. Not yet. The temptation is overwhelming though. Some moves invite it. There is also a move where you wind the follower up then unwind them fast. This is merry fun to do with someone with long hair. Every week with Katy - whether her mum is watching or not. We call it the helicopter. Katy introduced her new boyfriend one week and I guessed it would last about four. My compatibility assessment faculty was not wrong.

On the subject of getting too close we have a move that entails passing the lady's hand behind her back. This is ok when executed quickly, not so when done step by step. You find yourself bent down rather too close for comfort with your face inches from their breasts. Holding there while the teacher is babbling on. I pretty much refuse now. If I use the move, I throw the hand around behind them and grab it rather than exchange it behind them.

In a minute or two I will share some exciting details about someone who thinks they can dance to the music. I have seen a few people hit the beat. There are a few people that can, though they are few and far between. I gave my daughter two options. You can either take dance or drama. I don't care what subjects you choose in your school options, but I would like you to do one that is out of your comfort zone. She selected dance. She loved all the backstabbing, the rise of the teacher's pets, and general unfair unreasonable behaviour of the troupe. Unfortunately for me and her mother, we had to endure a couple of displays, displays that went on for an eternity. There was a spider monkey girl who would have been applauded if it was a gymnastics event. I have seen mice contort their body to squeeze through gaps, this girl could too but wasn't as furry. One by one, or four by four they came out to un-impress us. The seats were too uncomfortable to have a nap, and that was a good job as then I saw something that I was hoping for. Someone that can dance. She was black. I am not sure why I mention that as the colour of her skin made no difference to the way I judge the shear perfection of her moves. On the beat incontrovertibly. One out of sixty had natural talent and those that claim they can dance to the music need to emulate that before making unfounded claims.

I went to a wedding in a faraway place in Wales. So remote that there were queues of people at reception complaining about the lack of a phone signal. Here in front of me was a girl that defied belief. This was not hand to hand dancing I must point out. Disco dancing and messing about. I threw a jig, a jig perfected at many a rock concert. She copied. She copied in a way that was astounding. Every body quiver that I could invent was replicated with unfathomable dexterity. On her own initiative, she had exquisite control of her limbs, torso and all else. It was a marvel to watch. Some half-hour later I came to my senses. Off to the bar as no matter how impressive it is to see; one can't dwell too long in the company of those that are not over eighteen. If she didn't become some sort of professional dancer in the future I would faint with disappointment.

I have mentioned quite a few young dancers, but let's be clear, age is no barrier to great dancing. Some seventy-year-olds have excelled. I am sure there are many in their eighties that can hold their own. In fact, I have been more than impressed by the dexterity of what you might call long time pensioners. I have always danced with all. Religiously. I may specifically select a few to dance a bit more with from time to time given that I know their ability sparkles. One lady was a favourite. To add a needless descriptor, I will state that she was probably 55. We could syncopate. When I was focused.

When I say I pick out a few, I don't go overboard. Some do. You see them home in and take. They weave a distinct path from a start point to the plum berries. You can plot their route snaking around many idle options. All names have not been changed. I am not too good at remembering names as it is, so would be doubly pushed if I put in replacements. Some are inevitably misspelt. I make a point of not making effort to discredit others in order to make me look good. I also know that I am hypocritical to some extent.

Envy and jealousy surfaced, out of my body and into the ether when Laura arrived on the scene. Obviously, I am going to be making every effort to talk to her. No question of that. Some call it 'flies around shit'. That is not suitable so I will refer to it as flies around ice cream. I have Laura sitting to my left and we are mid-discussion about something or another. Then we have someone stooped over with their face close in front of Laura's. I am ignored and interrupted. He turns his head and motions to those on the dance floor. "These people can't dance to the music. .... but I can." This is flaming arrogance. It is also wide of the mark. I say to Helen later, "Apparently Arry can dance to the music", she responds with "Arry, dance, music - in the same sentence, no". He is akin to two telegraph poles welded to the ground with a workman repositioning them with a stumble shunt every five seconds. He does know how to make the women dizzy and gives them a varied workout. That is true. Not only has he made an egregious claim, but he has whisked Laura away from me for a lesson in 'look how good I think I am'. This happened many months prior to me panicking, acting in desperate need, and vying for the impossible. I have a good memory for this kind of bother.

More paragraphs of ink appear to be misused on this person. I will also remind you that out of some five hundred plus leaders that I have encountered, I have only had distaste for two, maybe three. And that is over many years at multiple venues.

It is bad form to refuse. A time out signal is less upsetting. If you decline a dance because exhaustion has set in, that is fine, but one ought to make sure you find them later and ask them for a dance when your batteries are recharged. It is hard enough for some to pluck up the courage to ask and it is made a lot worse being turned down. It is not nice. In my view, if you are going to a dance hall then you ought to be prepared to dance with everyone. My first refusal was near enough the only one I can recall. I found a way to limit them. She had brown hair, was attractive enough with a prickly porcupine personality. I have no idea why she had it in for me. Normally, it is because I have said something. I can't remember saying anything though. Nothing untoward for sure. No matter.

I changed venues to one that was ten minutes quicker to get to. I meet some wonderful characters. I would have many chats about writing and other things with a lady who seemed a bit too young to be retired but was. There was Millie and Minnie who took up dancing at an early age, dragged along each week, non-reluctantly, by their mother. Minnie was pretty good, Millie was pretty outstanding. The mother was one of the few that had a regular male follower, the first man I met that likes to follow more than lead. I would dance with Millie once a fortnight. She is young and I am caught between a rock and a hard place. Not dancing with the younger ones is silly, dancing too much with them invites raised eyebrows. All is fine for a year, until the brown-haired brat makes an appearance. All three of the youth team start refusing to dance with me. Great.

Two months pass and I am not sorry to hear that a condom didn't work as it supposed to. No more dancing for her for a good while. Whether in the spirit of Christmas or more likely the absence of that someone controlling their behaviour, normal service resumed. They will all dance with me again as if nothing had happened. I mention Millie as she was delightfully easily controllable, steerable and has the ability to interact flawlessly. I am pretty sure she went on to enter national championships. Thankyou Millie, thankyou Minnie, thankyou mother, you restored my faith in people.

Matt and Sarah are at the helm of an extensive franchise that I joined since moving to a new county. I decide to do a tour of all the pokey little ex-churches and village halls in the vicinity that offer up the same menu. Each have their own vibe and characters that impress plus folks that instil fear in beginners. One lady stopped me in my tracks, and not entirely helpfully, informed that I was doing it wrong. I may not have stepped aside far enough but I had done it over and over two nights prior. I do forget, but not this one, not so soon. A young lass named Siobhan sparkled. For a laugh I tried to establish whether she can cook. Beans on toast even. The teacher had plenty of enthusiasm for the genre. He would close his eyes whilst waving his left arm high counting us in. It was in a manner equivalent to getting an orchestra fired up. A lady did the cash collecting, although she seemed to pay little regard to the proceedings and spent most of the time on one of those infernal telephone machines. Nevertheless, she was notably pleasant to all. The thinness, sleekness and dapper nature of the teacher's follow-companion was noted.

I have seen you before said a local. I am sure that is not good, think I. A town not unfamiliar with flooding had not long finished the bulk of the clean-up from another high-water event, hence I asked about the consequences. She was here with her parents. She dressed in a way that represented a common theme in this era. It is neither feminine nor masculine, it is drab attire. I am trying to learn how to be less critical, but it is hard. The likes of she, are what makes one feel welcome and quickly included. They draw people there and keep them coming.

The next place had some strange roundabouts that lead everywhere except the hall. This is where I ask John to do me a favour and give Laura my number. A predictably pointless exercise of course. Hayley sauntered across to where I was standing, waiting, and reckoned that I looked like a rabbit caught in the headlights. I said it might be on account of her outstanding beauty. Hayley is ripe but the wrong fruit. Another less firm fruit seemed to be keeping her leftover dinner on her front to mop up later. A minx was also satisfying to talk with. You know within a few seconds whether someone is on your wavelength or not. However, casting aside our first impressions can pay off. Different people in different contexts can change one's view of them. My evaluation of the teacher here went up quite a bit. I had seen him hanging about on the sides in Matt's class. He was rather different on his own turf. He takes a more relaxed casual approach, but also takes the time to help those in need of it.

Years back I was goaded into going to a ninety-minute session of something called Zumba. A younger family member called Andy had suggested that it would be fun. In theory it was. We were the only two males amongst some two hundred women. Forget wine bars and pubs, this is where all the females hide out. The music boomed and we were invited to heave ourselves about briskly via silly ungainly stretches. Over and over. At a pace that wrecks the muscles with horrifying after-effects. I know horse riding can make your joints ache the next day, but this was ridiculous. To be fair by the third and final week it was not so bad. There seemed to be a few behind me that were excessively giggling. I had a feeling it had something to do with me dancing out of sync. Or doing cool disco bops. I know it is a little off putting. It not always on purpose, I find it hard to maintain the will to keep up with the rest.

I have been on the deck of a cruise ship and yes there is always one, me, that refuses to be a comrade in the communist line dancing fuddle. The DJ swings the light at yours truly and endeavours to get me to comply through isolative embarrassment. I give him the bird sign through the action of standing absolutely still, then tipping into a groove. I know I should try and fit in. At many a dance, a bunch of happy go lucky souls will do a convoluted formation step walk thing to certain tracks. Strolls. Sometimes I will see how many I can confuse with novel randomness. Usually, it is a cue to cool down outside.

I presume you are getting the drift. I like to mess about. I am an attention seeker and I love the spotlight on me. Just from time to time. I don't milk it. At one venue there were two of us that competed to act up in the most entertaining way. Tricky was a white-haired fellow with a permanent smile. When someone voiced his all-knowing opinion that Tricky should stop messing about all the time because the ladies don't like it. Tricky bellowed back. "I wouldn't do it if they didn't like it, you twat." One abiding memory was of Tricky being called to the front. He touched the shoulders of every woman in the line as he walked down. Each lady turned one after the other in a Mexican wave fashion. My name, Tricky's name are always called out by Debbie, every week. We are loved and loathed in equal measure. Tolerated mainly.

Most people are tolerated, but some are side-lined a little unfairly. Side-lined because of the impression people have of them. People get people wrong, regularly. My body is my temple, spend on good food and display your validity with some half-decent clothes.

There are some things that the followers can do to compensate for not being the lead. They can up the tempo, they can add flourishes and they can perform a few sabotages. I teach a sabotage to some women and goad them to do it with certain leaders. Essentially you will have the lady in front of you with your arms around her. The technical name is usually the 'basket'. She can then duck under your arms and pull away. It is best done without laughing or smiling. A serious face makes it seem as though they are doing what the leader wanted them to do. It is cool to do it on a near beginner leader, it takes them by surprise and throws them off completely.

The teacher is on the stage showing us step by step. Given that I know it is going to occur, I did what? You guessed it; I lowered myself down in time, preventing her from getting out. Up on-stage Debbie is entertained by me "sabotaging the sabotage".

As for upping the tempo, this can be a problem for the leader. There are some that seem to do a Zumba class and three hours in the gym prior to the dance evening. They are fit and fast. I do appreciate dancing with them but concede that I don't go out of my way to make it extra regular. A faster pace means you get very hot. You need to think much faster. You run out of moves quite quickly. Slow and smooth is more accommodating for me, sorry. Having said that, as the years pass and the number of moves I have at my disposal has gone up, I can accommodate it a lot more.

I want people to copy me. I like mindless 'trend setting' experiments. I will never know if certain people copied something that I did do a few times. Maybe I was not the inspiration. Nevertheless, I will always look back at this period, this past twelve months and see a grave error. Week after week people would say to me "I haven't seen you at the dances yet", "why do you not go to the band nights?", "why do the lessons and not go to the freestyle evenings?". They were telling me something. They were banging my head against the wall. I ignored them all. For heaven's sake Laura was going to them. I knew that. I had seen her link up with a marvellous couple, Sharon and John. At this point I have attended two band nights, rather belatedly. Had I gone right from the beginning, when Laura first ventured to them, it might have been a bit different. I assume I could have established myself at her table. I can't say with any certainty that it would really have helped, but it would have enabled me to glean vital information. I could have built up a rapport with her. Instead, I find myself well behind the curve. Crucial time was squandered.

Arry is having four dances with Laura to my one. That is liberty taking but maybe just me making a fuss over nothing. I do place myself next to her and talk. It is not easy, but I find a way to use up ten minutes through dialogue. I repeat this exercise at the next event. I can't keep myself there though. It doesn't feel right. The film 'Remains of the day' flash into my consciousness. Surely to god, this is not happening to me, I have seen such films. I have witnessed similar messages flash in front of me many times. Opportunities arise, they are presented on a sliver plater, and we do nothing, we curl up and turn inwards. Carpe diem, seize the chance or in my case leave it until the very last minute and be suffocated by the pressure.

A teeny bopper, a girl eighteen at most, maybe younger was only in the building five minutes before Arry was occupying her time. Half an hour later he was there for a second standing-nearly-still dance. Arms gallantly (ungainly) tossing her in methodical directions. She oscillated up and down at a pace similar to a freshly wound metronome. A good dancer but not terribly compatible with my pattern. In the same fashion as Millie would, she acknowledged my presence immediately and put her distraction device down straight away and keenly linked up with me. Now the bit that I am mildly perturbed by. He went over when she was alone and sat next to her. Maybe he was just offering her a Werthers original sweet and behaving like a caring great grandfather. It seemed odd, or me not thinking about the more serious events taking place in the world. The wars, the violations, the horrors, the abuses, the terrors and so on. In that context it is a miniscule aberration. Megan is expending thousands of calories being kept moving in reasonable synchronicity with her boyfriend. He is quite good. They have twenty dances. That is fine. Arry has two with her. Now what happens? You bet. The boyfriend has finally found the will to dance with someone else. So, the moment she is alone, Arry is parked next to her now. I had spoken to him a bit that night. "At least one thing about this dance lark, it keeps you fit", I said that to him whilst having an elevated body temperature. He turned his head and said, "I don't feel it". No more, I am done.

An accounts manager for a fruit firm asks me what I do. Now since I have begun to tell people that I am a philosopher I get one of two responses. They either ask, yes, but what do you do to make a living? Or they understand that lots of people make lots of money and the method in which you do it might not be as interesting as exploring the delights of humanity. We enter the realms of negativity. I explain that huge positives can spring from negative ideas. I gave her an example. The hang-ups relating to spreading our genes. Any child is only half yours. Your grandchildren dilute your genes to a quarter and by ten steps it is down to one thousandth. So, this can dispel the idea that it is vitally important that your seeds are the ones being used in reproduction. A foster parent, a stepparent can take great comfort from that.

Arry walks in, Laura is on the way out. He leans over to give her a kiss. She ducks and raises her arm. I refrain from kissing people at dances. If one goes in to kiss and they duck, surely you would back off and apologise? He carried on. Someone needs to have a word with him. I have not been there that long so don't feel in a position to make a fuss.

The flies around ice-cream issue will never go away in this land called England. In some countries the females are draped from head to toe in loose black cloth. I can see some tiny benefit in this custom. I have had endless trouble over the years starting with the misfortune of dealing with those that request threesomes. Asking for my partner to go to their house to fulfil a birthday wish. An ungentlemanly in-law called Phil didn't even consider some sort of reciprocity. Instead, he would corner my partner and make her feel most uncomfortable whenever she visited her sister's house. After that I had a friend suggest we play strip poker. Eh, without your wife here. Oh, hang on, you have split up. Then a wanker, another Dean, who said to my better half, "if you are ever passing and see my car on my drive, come in". I am sure plenty of other men have had to contend with this. So too have women on the other side of the coin. Some are unbelievably snide. One piece of flotsam called Mark plied my partner with a heap of vodka and 'invited' her to the bathroom. A timely reaction by me saved us both from a nasty sexually transmitted disease. The list of infractions never ceased until, well, until people become less of an object of desire I suppose. Steve, a recently divorced neighbour 'wanted some loving' as he was bereft now that his ex-wife had run off with someone in the police force. In Menorca, a try-it-on-with-anyone sat down and boasted about how many pesetas he had earned that night. Mate, England were playing, they won, tips were flowing abundantly. Tomorrow, you will have two coins that have been left on a table to clear up. Besides she, my partner, earns five times that. Every day.

I don't want to indulge in threesomes, nor do I feel inclined to have any kind of wife swapping activity. I never have. Plenty of others must do though. I was asked in a pub by a twenty something girl whether I would like a threesome. She pointed to the potential third party, she wasn't being serious, more to goad me. I replied, "you will be lucky". This went down like petrol on a barbeque. They were amazed. They were on my case for the rest of the night. I didn't have to say a single word thereafter. That was it.

What has this got to do with Laura? She has self-respect. What had this got to do with John and Sharon? Given that I have joined the table where Laura would be, I suspect that they had not realised who I was a tiny bit fond of. Laura was not there that night. John had his arm across the front of Sharon, hands between her legs, barricading her, persistently. I had a few brief exchanges with Sharon. I asked her for a dance and saw the look on John's face. Not 100% pleased. It is as if I am being very cheeky. He actually thinks I am sniffing around Sharon, oh my word. If I say I am not gravitated towards Sharon that might imply she is not sufficiently attractive. She is a giddy, always laughing, approachable sort, but not my cup of tea anyway. I am basing this on body language reads and could be off by a country mile. No, I am rarely wrong. I am insulted. I have no interest in your wife John. I know what it is like dealing with relationship wreckers. Whilst in the months ahead I had a few long discussions with Sharon regarding her dental nurse job, I opted to eschew any more dances with her to avoid any further friction.

I also can express a belief that having Laura around them, as a singleton, a treasure, is not perfect. Laura was 'with them' but not truly with them at this stage. I saw her at the end of an evening on the other side of the table, rather solo, leaning in to hear what gossip was being thrashed out. I made a point of saying goodbye to her and noted the not-fully-included position she was in. Group dynamics are complex though. It takes time to embed oneself. There was an instance where I could only watch on and had no licence to do anything. As the night draws to a close a song is played that summons all the women, mainly the women, to stand on the benches around every wall and they hoolah. Arms go up and chanting echoes around. Laura delays her rise to her feet. She looks alone. She is with everyone but not properly connected. I want to say, sod it, and go to her. I sense an obligation to refrain and can only watch. I don't watch her every move. Far from it, but I do spot key things. The difference between being there and really being there with her is profound. However, that was then, and I have another insight now. Laura is not a lonely individual. Not at all. This is just my romanticism. She is fully in control of her life. I would not have added a thing in that moment. I just had a belief that I could have shown some warmth. I am intrigued by Laura, and I am beginning to understand rather than guess what is going on. Only beginning to, though.

More and more men wear makeup now. Men have started to set foot into domains that have usually been only occupied by women. And vice versa. What has not been tackled so far? Long hair is not a potential. How about a ring. A ring that is delicate. I buy a nice small ornate platinum gold one and see what goes down - or not. I think in general it is so personal that people are reluctant to say anything. Only one, one lady does anything. She grabs my hand and inspects it, asking me what it is all about. I have something pre thought out to use for this event. However, it is rather hard hitting, so I decide to wait for someone else. It was a few months later in Greece. An affable buoyant skipper who was less inhibited than usual, probably due to the intoxicating effects of the punch, grabbed my hand in a similar manner. Studying the ring she enquires, "What is that?" I respond in a timely fashion, "It is on account of my late wife". Silence. She takes a few steps back. I end her short period of appearing slightly mortified by saying, "oh, I mean her period was late - and we had a child as a result".

As for the other cheap-as-chips item that adorns another finger, it has a quaint but timely philosophical significance. It is a 'ring for Ellie'. The one and only computer game that I have played this decade - one of the best ever produced. The Last of Us. It is a tale of two caught up in a proper pandemic. You control a pesky overbearing teenager and a chap called Joel. They unite over time, forming a co-operative father daughter type relationship. As you battle those that have risen again from the dead, you begin to get emotionally wrapped up in the drama. It ends with a scene where Joel scoops up Ellie and stops the doctors from taking lifesaving juices from her. It would be used to create a vaccine. She is immune, but in the process, it would end her life. Would I hypothetically behave in a similar way if Laura/Megan were vital for the current epidemic? You bet. So too for many others, but admittedly .... you know what I am going to say. Many were sacrificed in wars of the past in a similar vein. It is not quite as hypothetical as we imagine.

Matt the dance instructor has probably seen every move under the sun, many times. When he puts some of the things that I have been doing extra, into the curriculum, it is not exactly copying me. It is simply me reminding him. The third time it happened I am confident that it is me or very likely to be me, that is reminding him of some flourishes that can be added. Some call them variations. At another venue I spin the lady and spin myself on the spot as well. This variation was noted by the instructor. In this case he made the effort to ask me in front of everyone whether it was fine to use it. "I don't think there is any copyright", he says, but he wanted to check. A nice touch. I don't mind at all as it is nothing other than a way to tackle the tedium of most classes.

I am in the queue to pay. I am at this stage a real novice. I never get to be a fine dancer, but I try. When I really try, I am not that bad. I say something to the lady ahead of me. She doesn't agree with my statement. I am slapped down. When I have a dance with her utilising the limited moves in my pot, she decries one of them to be "not a Ceroc move". Not allowed apparently. It was a move I learned there, but never mind. The next week she moves down the line, to me. "Hello mate", say I in a welcoming tone. "I am not your mate." This is getting better all the time. After the fourth jarring event, I say something that is a bit off. I can't hold back. I say things sometimes that are not as cordial as they could be. "I feel sorry for your husband." That gives rise to a notable blank stare back at me. The next week I am beckoned over to the table and asked to sit down next to her. She is what you may call 'tidy'. Well turned out, in good shape and respectable. "About my husband", "He was on a bus in the city and was stabbed to death". We chat. We bond. We end up being rather pally. I sit with her week after week from then on and we get to know each other quite well. I can only imagine the life they had together. I am convinced she and her husband were true soul mates. I also get angry when politicians prioritise the welfare of those getting stopped and searched over the endless victims. We shift our focus away from the heartsore families with loved ones lost and concentrate only on the indignation of being checked for weapons.

There is a good reason for a particular habit of mine. Rather than approach a follower and ask, "would you care for a dance?", I stay out of earshot and use a finger to motion towards the dance floor. This has kept the number of refusals I have had down to about one. Sometimes a row of ladies will laugh, and they all replicate the same motion in unison.

She had gingery-blond hair, plenty of freckles and a nice complexion. Shy of thirty. Sitting at the front, close to the dance floor. For some unknown reason or perhaps because this girl had her back to me, I gave her a tiny tap on the head. I then used the finger motion as per usual. I am sure, very sure this was the only time I have ever tapped someone on the head at a dance night. We had a dance and as the music wound down, she said, "you mustn't tap my head as I have a brain tumour". Some six months later I see her arrive at a different venue with a compassionate friend. She was in a bad way. Her walk was ungainly. She was struggling. I led her on to the dance floor and the smooth slow style of mine paid dividends. Having never seen her since I wish her well and hope that the potential plasticity of the mind aids a bountiful long life.

I am sure these tales are worthy of filling precious moments with a muse. It helps express my belief that we are fragile, and we have to grab chances that we get. I never got to tell anyone these two dance stories. Besides, they would either have had no effect or an ill effect and could end up souring the mood. I will stand firm though and commend them never to be forgotten. They have a lasting impact on me. I felt for them truly. Given that interactions are often very brief we resort to quick jibes. When asked how long I have been dancing I sometimes reply, "about half an hour". It is eight o'clock in the evening, we start as seven thirty. "Where are you from?" "From my mother …. where on earth are you from?" I would glance at the bulky thing strapped to their wrists "You are *on tag*?", pretending that I have never seen a fitness watch before. One or two stopped wearing them after that.

I am now up late writing this stuff and remembering some black 'Christmas cracker comedy' relating to this plague thing. Why is it called a corona virus? It appears to be most catchable on a sun day. The sad demise of the victims seems to occur on their last day.

When people move down the line, we have a chance to get to know one another, ask what they have been up to, stare at the floor or whatever. I would immediately raise the lady's right arm, turning her. Then lower that arm whilst lifting her left hand turning her all the way round and back. That is my hello. Some, Michelle in particular, would stubbornly resist. I never did this with a beginner as it can confuse them a bit. It is also a bit bad as it separates the wheat from the chaff, those that I get along with better than others. Debbie of course would encourage us to "say hello and introduce each other with our names and not do a half nelson semi twirl". I carried on with the latter.

We break through the clouds, and I notice the unmistakable anvil clouds implicating a thunderstorm. The plane drops then jumps to the side making a good few of the passengers a little nervous. I have arrived in Helsinki to see my second Bruce Springsteen and the E Street band concert. A long one at just under four hours. I lost count of how many concerts I ended up going to. It must have been thirteen, fourteen or so on various tours of theirs.

I would arrive in the designated city a few days beforehand and view the sights. There was always an air of excitement. A justified one. What could be better? Favourite music, beers, and plenty of chances to have a dance with an array of women. You stand before a wall of sound that moves you. It is intense. For those conversant with the tracks, it is utter bliss. This is no stop start business. For the untrained ear it all sounds like one long racket. Each song will wind down a little before the next one begins. When there is a gap between songs it breaks the flow. This is crucial. The atmosphere gets interrupted. This band can play near constantly for the entire time. Understanding this became important when I want to build an equivalent atmosphere with someone. It is used when one dances over and over with someone all night.

In hindsight having you know who accompany me to these events would have been ineffable, beyond words. As it was, I interacted with a blonde. Not past her peak. She could move. She knew how to have fun. She was in fine fettle, Nordic and mesmerizing. She picked up the moves rather quickly. I was adding more and more, and she soon twigged the idea, just grab the hand on offer and go with the flow. After the third song I needed a brief breather. She inched over to where I was standing and there we were, side by side. "Everyone is watching us", was her concern. I had no concerns. As I looked around the stadium there were indeed a good few who were gazing in our direction. Holding their beer looking at us. Thousands more in the stands. All I care about is the fact that I am 'fraternising' with someone stupefying. I am not in dating mode. I really am not. The next track gets underway, and we set about doing more of the same. That was until 'out of nowhere' some gent grabbed her arms and despite her protestations led her off. I think he was given a ticket to ensure she was kept out of mischief. It was no boyfriend. Oops. No problem. Find someone else. People can get the wrong impression. All too easily.

The concerts highlight the utility of learning to dance. It gave me the confidence to hold out my hand and invite untold strangers to be extra happy for a few minutes. Australia, Auckland, Wembley, The Stade de France and so on. Arenas and pitches. I have been on hallowed ground in the centre of famous stadiums. One day I will go to a stadium to watch a professional football match instead. Perhaps to see our national team do something spectacular again, soaking up the atmosphere, the camaraderie, the noise, and collective joy.

I had a mooch to the front to compare the sound, there are sweet spots. Here at Wembley, I see a lady cavorting, dancing solo. I said nothing, I simply took her hand and engaged. A few minutes later I am off back to the where I was before. Short shared moments. The time, the place, the opportunity. You can speak through dance to someone in a way that a polyglot can't. It is a universal language, one small bit of leading and following says hello, nice to see you and all the best.

You can dance alone in your bedroom. You can dance with your partner in your bedroom. However, you can imagine dancing amongst sixty thousand people is distinctly different. At the front there are the faithful fans that go to every concert on every tour. They are crammed in, jostling, and soaked in the vibe. They form the choir. Some are not keen on crowd noises. I think it is wonderful. Thousands singing in harmony at certain points is moving. Further back, is me. I can move freely to top up my pint and scout out a valent vixen. For the music purists the arena in Norway was breath taking. Football stadiums are not designed for columns of speakers. It is hard for the sound engineers to deal with the echoes and get it out to all in equal measure. An arena can have the volume up a bit and even the deaf can hear via the vibrations rattling their chests. Bruce grabs a sign held up, a song request at random. Though I suspect the band chooses a miscellaneous track beforehand and rehearse it. Then all he has to do is hope that there is someone with the right handmade sign in the audience. It is theatre. Switzerland was not the same as Belgium. Nor was Manchester the same as Rome. But there was a connection between them all. People.

Hilo, Hawaii. Grab the chance say I to myself as I pluck up the courage to approach a sparkling lady. She takes my hand and with hollers of encouragement from her friends I show off what I can do in English persuasion. It was the last song of the night in that jazz bar. I didn't know it was going to be the last song. Thus, don't leave it too late. It is of course do as I say not as I do when it comes to an English dream.

Dancing can make boyfriends a weeny bit jealous. You see a pair arrive and park themselves down after the beginner lesson. The reason I identify the boyfriends and not the girlfriends stems from the lead follow divide. I have strutted my stuff with lots of first timers. Some get a bit flustered, some manage, and a few excel on their very first night. No boyfriend is going to ask someone to dance on their first outing. They only know two moves. They need to know twenty. They might have a teacher or taxi dancer give them a spot, but they are instead sat there watching the flies-around-ice-cream fandangle happen with their girlfriend. The cheek of it. I am sure some thought they would be just dancing with their partner. Some are taken aback when they line up at the beginning and were not expecting all the ladies to move down one, swapping partners. Some blokes can't resist impressing the newbies. Or at least attempting to impress them. There is also the novelty factor, but it is the impressing that stands head and shoulders above that.

Emma is a wiry cyclist that would have a couple of dozen candles on her birthday cake. I never got to dance with her much, as she left for the sunny south of England with her other half a few weeks after I joined the club. She makes a reappearance months later and I get her up. Her boyfriend gives me that look, that look of disdain and possessiveness. I imagine she makes him lump it or leave it.

I have to exercise caution at the concerts, but never got in any real bother. It is balance. These concerts are superb for me, they are superb for most others too except those that have not heard the music, a lot, beforehand. It is a barrage of sound that makes no sense whatsoever to anyone unfamiliar with the brilliance of it. Hence, inevitably you will either have the wife perplexed and the husband going mental or the other way around. He will be doing the 'dad dance' rollicking around and the wife looking on in amusement. Alternatively, it is he that is standing motionless whilst the wife is in the mood for it. This gives me an opportunity to play around. I will hold out the hand to the wife and run a few moves out. He is not unhappy; he gets a feeling that he ought to show some enthusiasm for the occasion. I never overdid it. I am soon passing her hand to his and they are improvising. You bet they bang like rabbits when they get back to the hotel – some outside 'interest' quite often sparks something.

The songs are stories, romance, tales of woe, coupling and connecting with people. Typically, a song will be written and performed. Released, played on the radio and danced to at a disco or rave. And that is it. This band did all that but then kept playing the same songs over and over, gradually improving them. As the years passed, the songs were transformed from good to great. Hundreds of tiny tweaks, deft shifts evolved something good into something remarkable. Each band member harmonised a little more to distil the sound into something refined. That was their magic that not many other artists copied to such a degree.

She had a nice maroon dress, long dark hair, and a distinctive face. Usual routine, hold out the hand and see if they will take it. One must never grab someone, absolutely never. Maybe wave palm up, a little bit to encourage, entice. She was quite good, but slightly self-conscious. Space in these stadiums, in some areas, can be limited with such vast numbers there. I tried to usher her towards a more open spot. More room is more flow and less chance of a bump into someone. She hadn't got enough confidence or had not downed enough alcohol yet for that. Too many observers. After dancing with her for a couple of songs, she vanished, and a lanky git appeared in my face. "You are good at scaring them off .... I had my eye on her." Oh dear. I just looked at him and he melted away, back to his mates. Of course, she came back. And we danced some more. Me being a 'fuck you' type made jolly well sure he saw us back at it.

I also continue using platitudes whenever I feel like it despite the admonishments in the past, as I am a 'fuck you' type.

My world view is markedly different to when I was younger. I used to believe that men and women were fundamentally different. I thought for example that women were better at menial tasks than men. I usually selected women for these dull jobs. When I offered these roles to some men, I was rather surprised. The lads stayed the course. They remained at my company far longer than I would have expected. They did well. Thus, my interest in equality and giving all people the chance to do what they want became a big thing for me. I did of course inform the candidates that the job was tedious. It was mundane and repetitive. If you let people know upfront, they will stick at it. It is better than presenting a misleading image.

Pushing equality aside we have the age thing. It is a big thing. It rears its head in most walks of life. There is generally more interest in those that have more years in front than behind them. We might believe that men want younger women. We might believe that men find the younger ones more appealing to dance with. That may or may not be true. That may or may not be prevalent. One truth is this. Women want to dance with younger men in equal measure. I have heard twenty, thirty-year-olds complain of the uninviting 'grab a grandad' scene that befalls some halls. We are all the same at heart. Nice looking men, nice looking women are beguiling. For me it is the juvenile-young behaviour that draws me in. That is found more often in the younger women. I think that is part of the reason why I got Laura's age wrong. She had a childlike tone. She acted beneath her years frequently. Megan could pass herself off as a seventeen-year-old on an Alan Turing test. You would either think you were on the other end of the line with an artificial intelligence machine or someone barely out of high school. Then you delve deeper and become confused as it would seem as if a forty-year-old was standing over her shoulder inputting things from time to time. That may at first glance seem a bit unfair if you take it wrong. In my mind, it is a perfect mix of youthful exuberance coupled with strong mature sensibilities.

Pam brought up the slight problem she was having with her knees. Me: "That is the trouble with getting older", "Say it how you mean it", was the jocular response. I realised that I have made fun of lots of people but never Laura. That needs to change. It takes me about five minutes to think something up. I have asked her out twice, she has turned me down twice, plus for some reason we had talked about musical instruments. I have a bass guitar, electric and acoustic ones too. I have had a coffin shaped box delivered from the People's Republic of China containing a wooden harp-type instrument. I have many more noise making items including a trumpet here too. Laura asked if I had a saxophone or a French horn. I lied. I said that I had a sax. I don't. I have all the others in the list I gave her. I was going to buy a saxophone but ending up not getting one. Rather than backtrack I left it at that. I did have a flash thought that were she ever to pop round my house I would have to run down to a music shop beforehand and buy one. Just in case she asked to see it. I made it clear that I play none of these things. I just play *with* them. She said she had a piano but can't play it. We are in the same boat. Though not a sailing boat yet. Anyway, the first thing I plan to say to her will be "Laura, I know why you don't play that piano. The only thing you are any good at playing, is playing hard to get."

A visit to a charming little village with plenty of those black and white, wattle and daub buildings, gives me an opportunity to drive very slowly back through torrential rain and countless ponds on the road. The storm is intense. One character decides to make his dancing reflect the weather outside. He is shaking his body about akin to a row of bean stalks rattling against the wall in the wind. All this thrashing bumbling has led to a romance with someone rather attractive. She has short wispy, light, alluring hair set around a very fanciable face. Her clothing is best described as vintage. There must be some charity shop that has a till full of her money and a volunteer that rushes to greet her each time she comes in to spend more. Her pleated skirt jars against her blouse. Thick black tights and make-a-quick-exit running shoes adds to my rude disquiet. The head that sits upon this concoction though, speaks of one word; covetable. The dances I have had with her were not great. That is my failing though, for sure. I will make more effort to adapt.

We played a game that was fixed right from the start. Souls that braved the weather and chanced their life to get there took a slip of pink paper that contained ten boxes. The idea is to get ten different people to dance with you. The best part being the faff trying to find a pen and then get them to sign their name on your sheet. I had already danced with nearly everyone there anyhow. One who inevitably got the applause and bottle of Tesco-sink-cleaner wine was a bit shorter than I first realised. She was focused. She was competent.

She took Megan's tongue thing to a new level. It was out trying to reach her earlobe. Height difference makes a lot of difference. Having someone that barely rises above your waist is unusual. I might be exaggerating a little here. It was announced that she turned eighteen that week. I would have preferred to have known that prior to asking her for a dance. It would have made me feel more comfortable.

On the subject of doing the rounds, I sometimes come across the slightly ungrateful beginner syndrome. One lady appeared to only get one dance, and that was with me. She sat there next to her husband. He ushered her up when I beckoned her towards me. He was there for her and her alone, for he never got the dance bug. It is nice that a partner will accompany someone to things that they have little interest in. Everyone assumes that we all know that they are beginners. It was not carnage I have to say. She followed very well. All was fine. As we parted, she said the moves are a bit complicated for a beginner. I do admit that sometimes I find myself thinking about something other than the dance in hand. I can pay no attention whatsoever to the level that the follower is at. I can be initiating moves that they will not have seen before even if they had been attending many lessons. In general, if you get the basic idea of following, you can follow whatever is thrown at you. Laura has said that I have confused her. I will take that. It is a neutral non-complaint.

Things can go wrong. Quite badly if you are not paying attention. Sorry Laura for the bump. It could have been my fault. She bashed shoulders with Michelle the artist. It may have been the other leader that was to blame. I will take responsibility though. Thankfully, no real harm was done. Once upon a time I stepped back on a lady. It was an ugly scene. I didn't cripple her, but it was evidently quite painful. I got scolded which in retrospect was not entirely fair. A second knock some weeks later and I noticed that it was the same leader not in control. I don't have eyes in the back of my head. It is the leader's responsibility to ensure collisions do not occur. Sometimes I find myself giving the lady a sharp pull out of harm's way. It disrupts the flow significantly, but it is essential that safety comes first. I have seen toenails lift out of place and 37 circles of blood make a trail to the side of the room. One follower was not seen for months after an incident. Touch wood - I have not be involved in such agonising scenes. I drilled into Megan the importance of this, and she became genius at pulling me out of the way when she led. I am not one for handing out advice, but there is a lot to be said for closed toe shoes.

A cool operator enters the building with a mission to impress. He does really well. Style, cascading swirls, and the arm up around the back of their neck to then flick their hair towards him. Four down and then the fifth was just not happening. It was to no avail; he couldn't get it going. She returned to her seat "What a load of shit, what a load of shit". He sat down too, and you could tell that the wind had been knocked out of his sails. He was crestfallen. He was impressive though. Take it from me, no matter how good you get, you can't gel with everyone. I have begun to aim for a fifty-fifty success rate. Some go very well. Most are so-so and a lot are ones where you are glad it is all over. It takes a while to adapt to each dancer. Not easy to accomplish in a few minutes with someone. Jo once said, "thank goodness that is over", to me. I then said "thank goodness that is over", every time with her thereafter. There are occasions where I feel that I am almost in the way. Each move is taking from what they are doing.

Thankfully, I have usually been able to join their groove in time and recover it.

If it is not going swimmingly for the dancers, the band singers can find themselves drowning. One singer had more belief in his skill than what the audience had. Laura said the band was "ok". Maybe that was how we got on to musical instruments. When he had muffled on for an hour or so there was an announcement that if anyone wanted to talk with him, get an autograph, selfie or whatever, he is at the side waiting. There wasn't exactly a queue forming. I thought about being his only customer. I was thinking of heading over and saying, "Hi mate, do you know where the toilets are?" He was after all mocked up to look akin to Elvis.

I have been practicing something that I failed to give a try when I was at school. It was invented in the 1920's I believe and made famous by an American singer. It is not complicated. I have seen girls online do it in a circle. Captivating to watch. It is bloody difficult though. Every week whilst waiting for my turn to take a shot at the pool table I practice it a bit. I play pool one handed. I am waiting for the day when someone challenges me to a game. I will say, "I bet I can beat you – one handed mate". After sticking at it for a year now, my chances are not that slim. Service personnel injured in war play one-handed golf, so I tried that then focused on pool. As for the dance move, I want to make sure that a certain lady is watching. Claire. She has made plenty of eye rolls when I attempt some flair with dancers in her vicinity. She sends ten too many hideous pulses, down her arms, into my spine as a way of counting in. In the line she reckons I have no tension. I wouldn't mind but she teaches somewhere. I'll find out soon enough on the tour. I did head in her direction a couple of times at a band night, to dance with her 'out of spite'. I was saved by the bell, as someone else got there first. Maybe in time it will transform into something marvellous. In the meantime, I hope she is extra unimpressed when I get to take Laura's hand and moonwalk into the centre of the dance floor. I only need to then top it off with some other show-off material. As for making an effort, I pulled a rabbit out of the hat with Matt's wife, Sarah. Given that Matt was manning the entrance and watching with interest, I ensured that it was better than my usual fare. There is a distinct grace moving in harmony with those that have been doing it a long while. Sarah in one word, authentic. Megan became semi-adept at this moonwalk with my encouragement, though I managed to beat her in each race.

So many unforeseen benefits are to be had from learning this Jive caper. I stumbled down some steps hoping for a one-for-the-walk-home drink in Budapest. This basement bar turned out to be a dancing haunt. As per usual, so long as you can lead, and they can follow it doesn't matter what strain of Jive has become established in that locality, it works. To get a shock and awe effect you can sit nonchalantly at the side then rise to the occasion and put on a show that no one would expect of you.

Three females in charge of the sailing flotilla were having none of it. No amount of persuasion would get any of them to oblige in a Jive session. Then a pre midlife crisis rocker waltzes in. She demonstrated her capability, fast and furiously with an accomplice. My turn. My head swelled to ever larger proportions when she exclaimed that it was the best dance she had ever had. When I left, she was sitting outside still swooning with her friends and said, "that was him there".

A skipper had fallen for an engineer whilst spending the summer working together. The skipper's mother happened to be a dance teacher. This may explain why she was so unexpectedly good at dancing with me - to the consternation of the engineer of course. I made him feel somewhat inadequate. It was a perfect way to get a micro revenge in. He then had to spend the rest of the evening doing a crash course in Jiving to save face. He was a bit of a lazy sod. The battery on my yacht was duff and he couldn't be bothered to sort it, nor fix the electrical cable to charge it when in port. This lead crew, skipper, hostess and engineer all share a dismal boat, rescuing us when in trouble. They had to put up with a lot of troublesome clients this year and more so on this particular leg. Some people are plain inconsiderate. I was good as gold of course. Maybe my five minutes with his girlfriend was something to cap off the season from hell. He wasn't that bothered really. He told me of the issues they had outside after.

The best room you have please. They hurried and scurried about to remove the cobwebs and sort out a working internet router. Few westerners had put this on a place of interest to check out. The room was splendid. It had some ten huge bay windows that looked out onto the dusty surroundings. A four-poster bed, a nearly derelict but working jacuzzi and space for a person per window. The best of it, half the price of a windowless room in Shanghai. We had a walkabout to glean what we could. There were two people bashing the crap out of some metal stuff in their house cum workshop. It appeared as though that was the norm for them all day, every day. I have lived in a ghetto west of Birmingham and have some experience of neighbours from hell. I assume they don't see it as an issue as such here, more life the way it is. At eight o'clock sharp the music starts, and all the locals congregate in and around a band stand. Some watch, some dance. One way or another I was intent on having a go.

I had had a rather nice dinner in the hotel restaurant beforehand accompanied by great-wall red wine. I asked about cake for dessert. They didn't have any left. "Go bake it, make it for us then, please." They did. They had serious concerns about the fact that it will take forty minutes or so to cook it. The chef kept popping his head out to make sure we were still at the table. It came. It was fab. The Chinese eat everything all at once. They don't do courses like us, starter main then sweet. It's a mouthful of cake followed by more cow tongue.

Alcohol is a best friend at times when trying to dance in such an alien environment. A lady finally relented and showed me how. It was a step this way twice, then three times that way, in close hold. We drifted around in a large circle with no end of whoops and surprises based on the sheer novelty of a foreigner joining in. It was all too reminiscent of when I first began Jive some years ago. I tried to get one or two of them to partake in some of my moves. They had a go for a few seconds and passed on it.

How hard can it be? You only have two arms and two legs. It takes many weeks to get to grips with the basics. It doesn't help if you turn up after an exhausting day at work. The mistakes I made, the mistakes others make at the same level of ineptitude are legendary. It is a pass it on thing. Not just one's cold and flu. People learn then help others do the same. There are two issues that I can identify that make it more challenging than you might think. If you have ever played with a remote-controlled car you tend to find it easy to handle when it is going away from you. When it is heading your way, it is much harder. Everything is reversed. I think the same applies when you watch someone demonstrate the move the opposite way around. Then you have the issue of constantly changing who you are dancing with every couple of minutes. Some will do it right. The next one all wrong. Then the next, somewhere in between. Make sure you have someone that knows what they are doing on your right. Otherwise, they will send confused partners down the line all night to you.

Having done all the beginner moves to death for some six weeks you are dubiously encouraged to have a go at the intermediate lessons. The comedy of errors begins all over again. You are also in a bit of a catch-22. This is a different catch-22 that I have been in with Laura. You know a bit, but not enough to get up and do some freestyle. You need to do plenty of freestyle to progress. A song lasts about three minutes. A complex sequence lasts twenty seconds. Thus, you need to know quite a few to make it through. Only one follower, Zoe, would agree to show me, aid me with a move to do. Nobody else. I had that dispiriting event where someone said, "shall we leave it there". Lovely. I suspect many people come for a bit then become disheartened. I reached a point where I could finally 'blag it'. Then it got easier by the week. One trick is to wait a good minute into the song so you have a lot less to do. Another is to have fall backs - simple fill in items.

As for Zoe. She came in and sat at the side. On what must have been her third week there, she was hailed from over the other side of the room by an admirer. Come join me. Shoulder length brown hair, petit and sweet was she. You could dance with vigour with her. She then coupled with the admirer's friend. I have seen a few people get together. There are though, many people that have partners at home and do not want to be troubled. A lady originally from the Catalonia region of Spain explained to me how it can be a minefield sometimes. Too many making advances. Now I am one of them. Sort of. Though Laura was the first I have ever asked out. And that was purely for the experiment. It is excusable? Do I think that it is in some way justifiable? I have been on the receiving end of it too. They are called two-flush floaters – they just won't go away. (A great line borrowed from a great writer AA Gill - now deceased.) The ablution material has borne out of living with someone for so long that mentions nothing bar toilets. After the most spiritual holiday she would return home and rather than tell everyone about how great things were, she would regale tales of toilets on trains that consisted of a hole leading straight down to the tracks.

One lady who did have some charms, some, not that many, would describe me as her favourite dancer. After four each evening at her pleasure and less mine it can become tempting to bend the no-refusal rule a little. Oddly, Denise said that she was going to try another venue in the new year. I said that I would see her there. I arrived to bed myself in with a new bunch of strangers and she was nowhere to be seen. A year later I get a happy new year message. My responding "What happened to you?", remained largely unanswered. I did kind of like it. Having those that flirted in my direction. I never responded. I had no need or desire to.

There is a slight, but key difference between me asking Laura out for a meal and dance and some that just want pudding so to speak. They are very different sort of pest that people ought not have to contend with really. Though not exactly my business.

Some followers can follow well, some less so. Some are like glued up skeletons. Some don't complete the moves. Some are floppy. Some are obstinate. Some take the lead whenever they take the fancy – not when vying for it. Some are uncontrollable. Some just do what they think they should be doing, paying no regard to the lead whatsoever.

I spent five important minutes with Laura early on. She will either deny or not recall what modicum of insight I gave her. It goes like this. We stand in front of one another holding both hands. I push and step back. She steps back too simultaneously. I pull and then we both step forward, legs together again. The aim of the game is to be both pushing, constantly, a little against one another. Not a lot but creating a coupling. Now with a little bit of practice I can push-pull over and over and we are in sync. I can stop at any point. I would stop/start randomly. She should hold fire and wait for the lead whether we are stepped back or stepped in. This is elementary and vital. Go try it and see how the simplest concept is at the whims of farcical miss-communication. Feel for it, focus and wait. Don't guess.

Imagine picking up an egg between your thumb and first finger. Splay the rest of your fingers out. When your arm is not being held, let it run outwards like a swan on heat. Place the back of your hand near to your cheek then circle-drop away. Make something original up. Do something, anything that suits your persona. Or just keep sleep-dancing for as long as you so wish. I am simply saying that you need not rest on your laurels. You can add things and spice it up if things appear to be getting stale.

I may have been rather unfair on some followers. So, I will be derisory about a heap of leaders too. I am only an average dancer, a dancer that could do better, so you are welcome to send nice comments my way too. These words about these happy go lucky triers is a polemic – my opinion.

Some try and emulate the hunch back of Notre-Dame. Many have a kind of Jive sickness that breaks out into a fever of sloppy stomps. I note the grins. Some have a pseudo-smile that reeks of unfounded self-confidence. Some pull out into an inverse grimace that is a way of congratulating themselves for doing a fancy sequence. Smiling intonates mastery. I dare you to smile lovingly. I challenge you to smile as a sign of pleasure rather than as signal showing a belief in your competency. Few will summon the courage to be seductive. Dancing is just dancing though, keep that in mind. One gesture can unnerve your temporary dance partner and their response will stick in your memory for eternity. We forget the hundreds of good dances and dwell a lot on the trivial number of ones that went wrong. I imagine this is why we end up being reserved and play it safe all the time.

The idea of making the girl look good is fine, but is that hiding laziness?

Every move can be turned into a lazy alternative. I resort to it if someone is keen to shift up a gear and I have not got the equivalent energy reserves. All one needs to do is maintain their momentum up and down the invisible tracks. You end up rotating rather than running about. The lady will cover 5 miles to your 1. Ladies, you can get your own back, take up lead sharing and you can then get the men doing 5 miles to your 1.

Someone somewhere made the moves up. They are not official. They are not set in stone and compulsory. You will be expected to keep it roughly in line with the Jive theme. Too much of a departure from the norm or being too progressive is not always welcome. They came to dance Jive not ballroom or Latin. However, some deviation helps people appreciate variety. Who wants the same dance with every person all night? At least half of your partners will value your individuality, the others will grumble a little. One or two will show dissent, but that is the price, the risk, that is worth suffering. Helen let me in on something that I didn't spot. Some leaders dance the exact sequence of moves every single time. That is unbelievable. I had heard that 'you know what you are going to get', but that is ridiculous. I might combine two moves regularly, but twenty! They must have taken the cue from their grandma who spiels the same story out time after time like a record on a gramophone deck.

Any fool can criticise, and most fools do. Whilst for many there is room for improvement, shall we say, there are many profoundly good followers about. So too are there comprehensively good leaders that are a marvel to watch.

Some leaders have a presence, a capability of taking the lead with the lead. They carve out a niche and dance with authority. Some followers set about dancing in a more disco dance manner. These are hard to tune to. You have a choice. Go with it, copy their jig to some extent or force the usual standard jive sequences on them. It takes experience to adapt to them and add to it rather than bludgeon your regular thing on them. Good dance is harmony.

The difference between a glued-up skeleton and a floppy one is frame. A stiffness is required to spin people and waltz. It is an area of dance that needs a hands-on approach to teach. Less demonstration and more one to one help with it is often needed. Essentially your whole upper body needs to stiffen up on cue. That way the leader can move the whole of you rather than just your arm.

I made the mistake of doing a lean with someone who I didn't realise had a bad back. It was a taxi dancer, (someone that gets in for free and goes around helping), so I would have thought they were in good shape. I found out later that one is supposed to ask if it is ok first. I do believe though, that how we reprimand someone is important. She made an honest mistake seem like a major wrong doing. You can do it in a nice way or do it in a way that makes one feel uncomfortable being there. Moral of the story? Perform leans only with those you know for sure are able to do them comfortably.

Sitting more than dancing are those that come along to support their partners. They have not got quite the same level of keenness or may not have the sprightliness to dance a lot. One such chap was quick to point out his age, 86, and how he was here on account of his friend. He recanted his world view and view out into the universe. An interest in science and ways of things was clearly evident. I didn't get the chance to tell him about my postulations regarding 'the only way'. Namely that there is only one way the universe can be built. So many characters join the dancing world from a broad range of backgrounds. Dancing is for everyone, everyone that gives it a go. Many are held back by shyness and self-consciousness. The more time at it, the more confidence you get. Confidence gained in dance can help in other walks of life.

Destiny my friends. If I change the word destiny to luck it can be less controversial. I took a long break from dancing and got the inclination to resume a few weeks before Laura began. I must ask her what spurred her to embark this ship. Did she speculate that she might meet someone? "You succeed in that", would be a good joke from me. So many questions. No time. Insufficient opportunity. Just imagine if Laura were to read this twaddle. I still wouldn't get those few hours needed without interruption to test something.

I am therefore just one of many hopers and dreamers. One more that wants more. One more that will never experience maximum fulfilment. Life is good, I know that. I say again, I have no complaints. Laura has given me dancing back without realising it. I have more energy now. I know what I am aiming for too. For a while I have found driving less of a drag. Before, a forty-five-minute journey seemed like a forty-five-minute journey, during this period it seemed like ten as I daydreamed and schemed.

This tale can't get any more farcical. Our Prime Minister has announced that we are not to visit any pubs, restaurants and such like anymore. I am very annoyed. He made this announcement at five o'clock. Why didn't he leave it until 7.30? Whilst everyone is worrying themselves silly about dying, I can only worry about not having another session with Laura. It is a demise of sorts. The end of what could be a good friendship. The dream of getting Laura to come with me on a sailing boat is drifting away. I turn up anyway along with a spartan crew of die-hards. We agree to do a pseudo-session. Carry on regardless. That is all well and good. However, I am not sure if luck is having a laugh with me. Whilst Matt is addressing us, Sarah pops outside into the foyer. I hear her say "hello there", in a warm startled fashion. She talks with someone; I hear the voice of the other party and half-believe that it is Laura. It would be the precise time she would arrive. I don't wish to be rude, so stay put. Why or why did I not go out and confirm who it was? Laura comes ahead of everything else at this point in time. Or should have from my selfish perspective. Laura does not make an appearance. I am dejected. I do an hour of dance with the other seven. When I get home, I think about the turn of events. Did she talk with Sarah and given that we were down on men, think it wouldn't be worth joining in? I will confirm my suspicions soon and feel even more aggrieved. Had I reacted I could have spent a few crucial minutes with Laura. I could have asked for her flipping phone number with a ruse about the state of the nation. I could do with a level head. I need an independent voice of reason to confer with. My level of pissed-off-ness has reached epic proportions. I may now not see Laura for weeks, months, or ever. An orange glow of Laura fixation has embedded itself in the front of my head. Sleep is not physically possible with it jammed there. I get about two hours of passed out refresh. In the morning I am dismayed. It is really bad now. Sick through my limbs. I could have spoken to her without others distracting us. If she had come in the dancing would be in large doses as so few there.

Some tears are shed. However, I am to get a positive from this hideous situation. Laura is having an unwitting influence. I must rewrite that infernal introduction to the book. I have been re-editing it for twenty years. I will dispense with the scoffing at the start. I will make it more readable. I will lay things out in a positive light now. Gloomy, down, depressed living alienates - not attracts.

This Laura lark is awful. I have a premonition that the next time I see her she will be smiling, and she will be extra happy. She will tell me the great news. She has found a wonderful boyfriend. Damn. I want to accept that it is a load of nonsense. That however is not possible. I have accepted the obvious reality. I am just not in the running. Not now, not ever. I never was likely to be. In truth she was a catalyst for change. I never truly wanted Laura as a partner, but she highlighted the sorts of characteristics that are most important. When I analyse it further, I home in on what I really seek. It is someone to go to dances with. Someone that I get on with, to have on hand, to explore dance at home and maybe even abroad. Laura would be ideal.

I say to my sister, "this is a not a good time for me, this lockdown", "when would be a good time?", she laughs/chides. Finally, I have a dance partner to work on moves with. It has been a long time coming. I also have Megan as a side hustle too. Two great people and what looks like an eternity before I can exploit it. Of all the things that will be legally allowed to resume, dancing will be the last thing. I am peeved. I write a few lines to Megan. She has plenty to keep herself occupied with and is making good use of the time. She seems quite accepting of the lockdown. I am not, but out of caution I say nothing.

Some years back I watched Mille and a DJ dude formulating sequences. They would put the odd novel part in with it. They practiced a little each week. As I looked on, I said to myself, that is what I would like to do. The only thing stopping me was having a co-operative consort. They are hard to come by. I finally get one, or in fact two really, and then bang. All evaporated. This is most annoying.

No more Jive for a while means no chance to play a prank on Matt to get him back for pranking us. I have the perfect prank lined up for him too. His prank went like this: I have Laura to my right as a spare. I half think that she may jump past me given the events earlier that evening. I have done the routine twice with the partner in hand, so now it is "one lady on". Nope. "Again." What? Once is typical. Twice sometimes, but three times? For heaven's sake. As said before I want to know if she is alright with me. Fast forward a couple of weeks and this time I see Matt look at Laura and then look at me then grin. Lo and behold it is not, "one lady on", but as you can guess it is "again", instead. For a third time. No offence to the wonderful person that I was with, but I have done the whole routine twice already with them. This is using up precious time. I have things in process with Laura.

There is always someone worse off than you. That may be so. Yes, some are stuck in a flat. Some have lost their job. Some are struggling to breathe. Some are in hellish pain. As I sit in the sunshine in my acres of garden and enjoy the extra quiet, I am writing about my anguish ignoring the ones who are really suffering. I just can't help but think that this would be rather bearable if I could see Laura once or twice a week. There is absolutely nothing to look forward to. Lots of so-so things. Curiosity inflicts displeasure because there is no certainty of when things will brighten up. There are too many unknowns. No consensus. We can't say that in three months' time or x months' time it will be fine. I suspected that rioting would begin. Thankfully, it didn't. Never mind. Keep calm and barely carry on. Sixty million people losing one year of their lives, counts for little. 600,000 people die each year, their last year is hardly fun for them. I am sure far too much has been written about this pandemic. I will delete this part later. As will I delete the fantasy too.

I pounded the streets with a protest board after four weeks of being put under house arrest. Exercising. I was the first in the UK to protest and a lonely figure. No one would join me. No one would even hang a sign outside their house showing their discontent. I 'incited' plenty to do so. I had hundreds of thousands of people watching my campaign videos, but they had such an impact that not one person would brave it. I stopped in the centre of the city and begun to talk to various lemons walking about. Many agreed with my stance, one thought I was a 'berk'. Not only have our human rights to see friends and family been taken away alongside our right to work but also our practical right to protest. Two women from the council made a bee line towards me and insisted that I was not allowed to stand still. They are made up of 90% water and 10% pure evil. They didn't like seeing a crowd gathering, albeit a small one as there were not many people about to protest to. They said I am on CCTV. "Send the footage to the BBC." They could not care one jot that they are complicit in what I see as a manslaughterous vile lethal lockdown. They are following orders.

Everyone is following orders with no debate allowed. The one thing that held me steady throughout was the fact that operations were being cancelled on a grand scale. This would have consequences. The vast sums of money spent could have been used to save untold numbers in the years ahead. I had many internal conflicts. Was I right? The government's line sure was convincing at times.

I wanted to see Laura again. And see her again I did after a bit of searching. She was in her garden meddling with what I thought were vegetables. They were in fact flowers. "Hi ya", was the barely warm welcome that I got. She brought out a cake rack, full of nice things to eat along with a cool drink. It was one of the hottest days of the year. Not really. She offered me nothing. I gave her a small plastic box of chocolates that she grudgingly accepted. All she wanted to do was hand me back the coin I'd sent her and wash her hands of me. Her house was rather nice with a good bit of ground around it. She showed me the place with pride. Not really. She showed me the car park and then the exit. I get the hint. I won't return that is for sure. We had a nice decent chat though. She warmed a good bit as the conversation went on. She had been active. She had helped her father on the annual better-than-the-gym hay gathering task. She looked cute. I could see now that she looked thirty-six. How I managed to convince myself for so long that she was thirty I do not know.

I was 99% sure Laura would be fine and not suffering too badly with the state of affairs. Kaye, my cleaner, seemed ok but wasn't. She took an overdose. Thankfully not fatal. Three dear people I knew very well killed themselves. Winfred had not taken the bull by the horns and let a chance of happiness fall by the wayside. I worked for her doing various gardening duties for some time. Had she married the love of her life, she wouldn't have had that regret eating away at her for all those years. She jumped into a river. A young man got a medal and recognition in the newspapers for jumping in to rescue her. A week later it was concrete that ended the depression. Mark was a shock. I knew he was in a lot of money bother but couldn't believe it got to him, so much that he ended his life. He worked for me for a few months and seemed full of promise. A handsome lad. Lyndon was in the same year as me at school. He came from a religious family. He had cheekiness, exuberance, nerve, and character. His father disowned him on his death. Quite extraordinary all round and clearly, sad. Lots took their own lives during the lockdown as life became such a struggle. People fail to understand how people feel. They think it is selfish and hurtful to the families left behind. It is, but the dismissive nature of people's attitude grates.

Laura said she was stressed out. Her message was garbled. Some say they are doing ok but are not. Checking she was fine was not the only reason for going around to see her, but an important one. There were two Laura's on the index. This one was too old, but I had to check it out. When I found out it was the right one, I had to see it for myself to believe it. Without her makeup it was apparent that an age miss-gauge was true. It is hard to let go of a belief. I really thought the other Laura was the dancer that I was looking for. In my day before mobile phones and all that we went around to see our friends. It was normal. We didn't write them a letter and wait a week for confirmation. Lots of my friends would turn up from time to time, knock on the door and they came in for a cup of tea or spliff.

An opportunity is opening up. Whilst it is fantastic to be able to dance with all, a few months with just one person, the right sort of person is tremendous. The scope of what we could cover is enormous. We could syncopate. We could learn to read one another instinctively. Dancing would be super splendid. She could learn the lead with me, and we can then move on to the sharing. She is a lean mean dance machine that needs pushing to the max. She has untold potential that has yet to be exploited. I could make her into something outstanding. I have seen it before with graduate Beth and various others. All it takes is time to draw out the passion. $1 + 1 + x$ = magic. X being the music. I know Laura is not driven by the 'ok' fare at the dance events. I have danced at concerts, in all kinds of places where the sound from those speakers sparks paradise. If it has to be Motown, then so be it, if that fires her up.

A meet up of the dancers was announced. I went with the expectation that I would get a frosty reception. I had hoped that Laura would be there. She had mentioned that she had met up with some of the others a week or so ago. Nice to be invited. Maybe they were dancing too? Who knows I thought afterwards. I was in for a shock. I was invited to join Helen, Denver and Maureen on their table. It was nice to catch up. All others were in great spirits, pleased to see one another again. But most unexpectantly, they were dancing with one another. We entered a strange phase. Some are willing to dance with all, whilst some are wanting to limit how many they will dance with. Do I ask? We don't want to put people through that saying "no, sorry", over and over. In dancing we never refuse but these are stupid times. Jo is great. She assumed that I was limiting my contact and I thought the same of her. We were both wrong. At some point we Jived together in her e-type jaguar classic style. I sit outside and listened in on Sophie who was regaling a tale of hot things in the kitchen. One burnt her foot. The other was someone she was lusting over – a overly handsome employee.

I needed to explain something to John. I had chosen John Smith as a pseudonym for the dance video conferencing. I could have used Joe Bloggs, but it was John Smith. I debate controversial subjects. Genders, equality, lockdown deaths, philosophy etc and feel it better to have an alias. The dickheads that come out of the woodwork ranting about their misinterpretation of the many twenty-thirty second videos I make is unreal. Others have had to hide behind tall walls as people get aggressive. Anyway, there was some ten or twelve participants taking part over the weeks on this video dance thing. And one of them was actually called John Smith. I thought at first, he was copying me. Not so. If it can happen, it will, so it says in one of Murphy's laws. Laura reckoned she wouldn't get much out of it. I suspect she would have had her fill of video meetings in her job.

Dancing is to resume, firstly with some test dance nights and then classes shortly after. This is great and ghastly. There is a super snag. Everyone needs an exclusive partner. This is an opportunity of a lifetime. Just imagine having Laura all to myself all night every week. Then there will be social nights with her too. Nothing could be better. The only small issue is persuading my dear Laura to "bubble up" with me. Having her as my dance partner for the foreseeable future is profoundly exciting. I can experiment to my heart's content. This is gold dust. As you can guess it will turn to vacuum cleaner dust. I had tried gaming her. I had tried persuasion. I had tried all kinds of psychological tricks. I tried pleading to her sense of reason. I got exasperated and in the heat of it I sent a message that had an ill effect. I said that I was devastated, and the piano joke was tagged on to the end of the last message.

I want someone that is keen to lead. It is not that easy, even for a little practice. Jo had said I was too awkward and wouldn't lead me anymore. On top of that, most have already formed bubbles. There is Megan though. "How's the bubbling up going?", I asked. "Hi lovely .... I would love to bubble up with you", came the reply. A lesson to you people. People read the beginning and the end of messages but often skim the middle. Put the important stuff at the start and the end. I skimmed the bit that said, "I have a partner that may want to learn to dance". The claps and air punches of joy faded fast on the second proper read. Shit. I have no one. All I have is an unsightly option to do the solo class. Strolls. Utter shit. Maybe Laura will be there? Not quite so shit.

Jo found me awkward, what she meant was that I was a heavy follower. I resisted too much. The best followers can be steered with the lightest touch. It was a while before I became easier to manhandle.

It is summer and the central park is full of us Jivers throwing caution to the lack of wind. I talk with everyone and dance with plenty. Three weeks on the trot. No bloody Laura though. I see what looks like Megan in the distance. Is that her? Has she got a wig on? I tell her that when I have a brief chat. She is in full lockdown lunacy mode. Total paid up member of the anti-social distancing club. "Better than some of the comments I have had", she said smiling at the wig comment. My sense of entitlement is evident in my disquiet about the situation, the Laura situation. I may have been unfairly confrontational if she had been in the park. This turns to contrition soon after. I feel I have done a little wrong.

If I am going to say it to one person, I will say it to all. No talking behind people's back for me. Debbie walks in (the dance teacher), wearing knee length cowboy boots. "Has she been horse riding?", say I to two gents next to me. "I bet you wouldn't say that to her face." "Debbie ... have you been horse riding today?", "Oh no I have these on because blah blah blah". I did have a reasonable dance with Debbie and after I said, "you're not a bad dancer", to which she replied, "well I am a dance teacher". My jokes often fall flat.

I get a tip off. There is a secret dancing society with exclusive membership taking place each Wednesday evening in a small country village pub. I was given the wrong pub, but Laura's car is in the street. She is here somewhere. I considered making some excuse to go into a restaurant to see if she is in there. Anything to see her. Then I spot Hazel. I say hello and follow into the right pub. The exclusivity is justified as the dance floor is not much bigger than an upturned table from a large manor house. Laura exhaled an "oh no". I presumed she did anyway as this was confirmed by the daggers and look of disdain whilst we were near each other at the bar. Upon talking to the barman, I discover that it is John's pub. In the family since 1663 or thereabouts. I look over at John who had Laura next to him obscured by the woodwork and intonated, "Your pub?" I needed some courage that I never usually need to go over and nestle myself next to this lean mean dance machine.

She looks up at me then stalls, fixed there, eyeballing me. I ask her about her walking trip on the Welsh coast. I sit down. Then gradually edge closer. I have two aims tonight. Talk and have a dance. I reason that if she dances with me tonight, she will find it much harder to decline in the days and weeks ahead. The hour and half passes quickly. We converse. Laura can converse. No diatribe, no dull one-way discourse. All is fine. All is well. I drop a philosophy item on her. I told her I had 'made' some clay from the earth on my land and was fashioning a sculpture. It was an illustration of selfishness. A mother with leaking tits. Pour water in the mouth and the belly fills then overflows out of the holes in the handcrafted breasts. "A mother can't feed a baby unless they feed themselves. We have to be selfish", I recount. "I suppose so", says my little Laura. I call it co-considerational selfishness. It is wonderful and not bad at all. You have to eat and drink in order to lactate the milk.

I leave. I return the next week. I am hoping that I can build upon the niceties of the week before. I am of course drawn towards where Laura is sitting with less hesitation. She is not overjoyed to see me again. John looks at me then Laura. It has all turned to mush. Has something happened? The conversation is really strained. I find out a bit about her university travails and some other innocuous items. She is not fond of me now at all. The week before I had pressed her hard to dance. I asked, I said nothing whilst she clenched her mouth and cheeks in by the cheekiness of the dare. She of course relented. These sales techniques always come up trumps. We danced in a humdrum perfunctory manner. It didn't matter. It was a dance, and it was the only dance I had or wanted to have that night. All the others can wait. I must not occupy the tiddly dance floor and get in the way.

I brought John a bottle of prosecco, sand to the flipping Arabs, as a gesture of thanks for making me feel welcome the week before. I told him as much at one of the dance in the parks. I have many peculiarities; one being - showing gratitude after the event whenever people display niceness. Tonight, I have sculptress Michelle asking me for a dance, briefly checking whether Laura wanted to. Laura was not hesitant. Go ahead, be my guest. Sometime later I ask, "hold my two hands Laura and see what you can do". Lead anything. This is a great exercise. Forget the steps. Forget any proper way of learning stuff, just think, and craft. She excelled. She moved me about, got us both in all sorts of knots and untied them. There are quite a few ways to shift someone about whilst keeping hold of both hands. I like looking at the faces of those leading for the first time. They grin and gurn as they puzzle out what to do, with Laura frowning once or twice too.

Laura had apparently led many times before. Or so she was quick to point out after I hinted that maybe that was the first time. Of course not. I think Laura has led when she was supposed to be following rather than leading in true fashion. Who cares. She is getting ever more grumpy as the night wears on. She gets up and has a brief exchange with Sharon outside. The second time she gets up she turns on her heels and looks down at me to say goodbye. "Goodbye (you contemptuous schoolboy)." Nothing surpasses the patronising sneering manner of a public-school teacher. She is a posh-school teacher - give me a detention Laura. A two hour one. In a fine restaurant. This was not long after her saying "NO". I had gestured to her to do the same dance exercise but with just one hand instead. In a softer tone, "I want to learn it with the steps. .... properly".

I hate properly, but I liked the fact that she quickly softens. It is a powerful and exemplary way to handle these sorts of things. I was asked decades prior when I was going to get a proper job. Presumably, a job that paid a quarter of what I was earning and a quarter of the fun. Laughably, Sarah a flat mate who asked me this got made redundant from her proper job a few months later. They performed the redundancies in a proper fashion. They made the manager sit down with each employee and tell them the good news. After a full day of that fun, the manager was sat down and told that he too was made redundant. That is the proper way to do things.

Laura is not happy. Or to be fair, not happy with me. Not in the slightest. I am perplexed. What have I done? Last week it was all good. I am upset that she is upset. It was only a matter of time before she snapped. I had anticipated it. I had been badgering and hectoring her a bit to get her to oblige in bubbling up. The upside to that was so huge. I was to give her a high five and say "finally". It took me by surprise though and I didn't respond. When we were kids, we put a can of beer on a campfire. We waited and waited. As we were just about to give up, floosh, up in the air it went. That's Laura right there. I think she tried her best to give me enough hints and decline in a pleasant way hoping I would give up.

I did read the news before I set out that evening and the omens were not good.

> Hurricane Laura batters the Louisiana coastline with an intensity the region has not seen in over a century
>
> Madeline Holcombe, CNN
>
> Updated 7:49 AM EDT August 27, 2020

Anyway, I have an idea. How about I send her some yellow roses. That will smooth things out, I'm sure. I was quite sure of it until Laura walked with purpose. She walked right into the dance hall to the WC. Then meandered like a stream around my aura to the furthest reaches of the room. I slowly sauntered down to stand next to her. I stay next to her. We have a government that decrees that one shall keep a randomly assigned two metre separation. She has plenty of options. Look straight ahead for an hour is the only one. I approach and begin an apology. Though I am not really sure what I am apologising for precisely. She stands at a quarter turn in defiance, defence. She says nothing much. She then abides by another well thought out rule, namely leave by the side door rather than the main entrance. This hassle might extend the torture of the lockdowns and delays deaths by a few more days. Or have no effect at all on the spread of a not-that-deadly virus. Ebola is deadly. As are all kinds of dangers. Broadly speaking, this thing tends to hasten the demise of terminally ill people. That is the way I see it in nine of out of ten cases. Old people. Average age 80. People on borrowed time.

People who have lived on average ten years longer than those in my youth, the 1970's/80's.

I follow in hot pursuit and catch up with her outside the one toilet in use. "How on earth did we get here?" "Stop sending me things", "Things?", "I only sent one thing", runs through my head. "Oh, you got the flowers then." This is real bad. It gets worse the next week. "Stop sending me messages." She has brought the coin in the box to give back to me. I decline. "When I have explained things", "I think you have explained enough". She grudgingly pops out to put it back in her car. I take my position in the silly strolls a few ladies down. Matt notices. The room is packed. Less so each week thereafter until just eight stick it out. Laura only does four weeks. I endure all eight. I can't get into the second part. The dance with a partner part. The whole point of Jive part. Laura has a partner. I am not sure who. If it is a certain someone, I will be furious. It transpires to be Jo. That is ok-ish. I need a way in. I refuse to form a partnership with anybody. I don't want to be stuck with someone that I can't express myself with. I want to learn the follow. I want to push forward with lead sharing.

I have come to terms with the egregiousness of this spiteful lockdown shit show and the third partner dance night beckons. I have missed two and may have to miss twenty-two. Maybe a hundred and two. It is depressing. It is no fun. It is sad. It is frustrating. My media campaign against the lawless government is gaining traction. This is the only release. I scan the dance message board. The message board for the losers, the dejected relegated few who are in search of a partner to conjoin with for the approaching winter of discontent. Lo and behold young Megan has put herself up for some hapless drool to team with her. She is bound to have heard about the shenanigans with Laura via Jo, hence has not approached me. She knows that I am more than willing. She has dumped the latest of her 'boyfriends'. She writes (shaved hair) in parentheses so that we all know full well who she is. I am two days late to this announcement. I drop her a line and wait. I don't want to wait days. She has always responded quickly to other messages. This is more despair. I write another line. "Sorry, I should not have asked." I think I put her in a spot of don't-want-to-say-no but also don't want to upset either. Alas I do get a response. "Yes, that would be great."

Week three of the party of those with and with those without left in the cold. I am strolling of sorts fully out of sync with the other line dancers even further away from Laura. I need to give her some space. One lady smartly dressed in mid heels and thick tights stinks. I wasn't quite sure who it was at first. It was only confirmed when she moved out of a crowded zone. She was the only clown with a mask on. I have had an odour related issue myself on an occasion when deodorant ran out. I had loaded some heavy stuff from the car into storage on the way to a dance night. This lady though was overpowering from over and above the two-metre invisible fence. A talked to her a bit. Maybe she would become a regular feature of our dance circle in the future. I hope so. She was sleek.

Out the side door I go. I don't look at Laura. I hadn't spoken to her. I had only shouted out that a lady with long blonde hair was the best. Laura was not charmed by that. Laura was the best. She did the arms spanned out and bum wiggle in a so-bad-it-is-good rhythm each week. She could do the Charleston with grace. She was plum to watch. Annoying that I can't take her hand and swirl. I wait in the car for Megan. I am confident she will show and show she did. In I go again. Laura is a long way down the hall and glares at me. "What. You have to be kidding", she intonates.

I lead Megan for this one initial night. I put her in an over shoulder 'basket' after completing the move in process. I hold her there. Matt looks, looks again. "Have to watch these two", as all the other dancers are in a different correct hold. Laura must have said "what a prat", to Claire. Claire had volunteered her services whilst Jo was away. I mention this for Claire has once said, "You are not going to do that Ceroc shit are you", to me in the past. That just adds to those eye rolls on countless occasions when I moved people in ways that are not in the rigid book that some adhere to. Claire and Laura together. Great. I do like Claire though, 'she is alright'. Being a dance teacher herself at another hall, one would expect encouragement rather than disdain. Other men would walk. (By the way, Ceroc is not shit – far from it.)

Week four, second time with Megan and her reluctance to lead needs to be overcome. "You can do it." And do it she did. Quite well. Though we are struggling. Basic moves take us an age to get vaguely right. Megan asks Matt how well we did the following week, she needn't have. We were not great Megan. Crap in other words.

I keep catching her in places one ought not to when she is leading. She was not fussed in the slightest, but I am a bit. I raise the issue and she is distinctly not bothered by it. Still, something must be wrong somewhere. It dawns on me what the problem is. She has her elbows too far back. They must always be kept forward of your centre line. With that sorted it solves that problem and her leading is sharper.

Week by week we make progress. Week by week we bond. Week by week things are on the up. Each week I get a tiny opportunity to speak to Laura. A week is a long time in politics. A week thinking about how I can use a few moments to bring Laura around drags. I just want peace. Get it out of the minus, negative zone back to zero. Social dances provide some interval from the pain. For the first time in a long time, I am now going to these evenings in a group. This is nice. It is more than that. It *is* nice. I wait outside having arrived before her and Helen. They call out my name. I enter with them. I am with them. I have failed in the past to build myself into a group. I could have done. I should have done. Now I am in a little tight knit bunch. It is pleasing. We are with umpteen Colins. One likes super slow Jive. Having seen a lady at 106 still dance it gives us cause to celebrate that whilst we may slow down, we never need stop.

Jo said she was apprehensive, scared to go to the dances on her own. I was not in the least bit scared, but it is not great. You are in a hall with a lot of people but feel alone. You are up dancing soon enough, but you return to a table isolated to a fair degree. Once you get into a group that all changes. There are cliques and people are welcoming but not super welcoming. I have always found it hard to choose which group to bed in with. Evidently, I made a mistake in not joining with Megan and Co earlier on.

I tried a silly test the once. I sat there at the beginning waiting to see how long it would take before someone, anyone would ask me for a dance. Forty minutes. It was the friend of Steve's girlfriend, bless her that got me out of my slouch, "I haven't seen you dance yet". The lady I was sitting near was surprised – not as shy as I might look.

That exercise won't be repeated, I worked my way around the room one by one. Some sit there waiting. I can't say I have ever seen Laura ask anyone. Though I have seen some that needed to take a deep breath before heading over to ask her. They have paid the entrance fee and want their turn.

If I am going to be honest, I put more effort in when a lady comes over to ask me for a dance. I try to make it feel a little more special in recognition of them making the effort to come to me.

If you get too good, some will feel as if they are not good enough to dance with you. I have been told this occasionally. Totally ridiculous. It is not about how good you are; it is all about your attitude. We have an obligation to dance with as many different people as we can and only dislike grumbling, whinging, and moaning. I personally don't care how crap you are or how crap you think you are. All I care about is how keen you are. Most leaders will go through a move with you if you want to perfect something. They are glad to help. Even right in the middle of a heaving throbbing dance floor. It doesn't matter.

I attempt to lay out the foundations of what I want to do in between fairly standard dance routines. I ask Megan to stand in front of me and fall forward. Once leaning forward and supporting each other, one of us pushes us back to upright. We then try again a little further apart. It is a trust balance co-operation test of sorts. This distraction provides minimal amusement for Megan. Each thing I try, garners ever less interest. However, things are more than so-so. We have small talks. A good few of them. I am not struggling but neither am I getting a sense of anything special. Then the gender problem, the multifaceted gender problem surfaces. She says that her dad often says things just to wind her up. She has a handle on the complexities of the gender situation in society that impresses and surprises me. She is also sitting at an angle in a body-language-tells-all manner that is welcome.

I think to myself what a wonderful world this is, but what I need to do is up the game. I need to show Megan what dance is all about. I had considered putting a power track on by means of a request to the DJ with Laura. Then I can dance with purpose. I opt for some headphones instead. Expensive ones. One for each of us and a gadget to make it work. I pay extra to have them delivered in time for Friday. I set them up and get some music organised. I head over to the dance night in a rush of sorts and enter with great expectations. I look down the dimly lit room and thought Megan was down there sitting to have a bit of a talk to someone. But it is not her. Helen tells me that Megan is not coming. For fuck's sake. I make no attempt to hide my disappointment. Helen has three blokes to dance with. Three to keep alive. I slumped into my seat and drown myself in a mini bottle of wine. I got no message from Megan. I got asked stuff by Colin that I am not really bothered about right now.

My mind is elsewhere. She probably won't turn up on Monday either. The evening wasn't so bad. I am grumbling unfairly. As the night wore on Helen made it all worthwhile.

On the way to meet some friends a message vibrates. I pull in to read it expecting some bollocks, but it is an apology. "Lady things", and an assurance that we are to dance at the class tomorrow. That is a relief.

She looks puzzled. She looks confused. Her face spoke of perplexment. She has just had two dances with music at loud volume bashed into her eardrums. A Springsteen track and something else. No time left for more. The enlightenment began here. The following Friday was a showdown. The song starts with, "Take your hands, my dear, and place them both in mine". She gives me a look of what the fuck. Then goes loopy. Jumping. I have a crazy in my hands. An utter nutjob. More ultra-modern happening super tunes. Loud. Thumping beat. A departure from the centuries old dreary tin pot medleys that has been the background to the dances for her past 9 months in the Jive scene.

The bop has gone. We enter the method of me. Smooth flowing and speed adjustment. Very fast then bang to a virtual stop. Changing paces, changing grooves, changing dances. Boredom is nowhere to be seen. She remarks, "I feel Euphoric".

It was the coming together of the past and the present. Her parents were somewhat surprised that she had opted to take up Jive. They had witnessed her dancing like a man possessed for years and Jive is somewhat more sedentary in comparison. Now she can dance like a man possessed integrating Jive moves. The two incorporated more than doubles the exhilaration.

We can dance to any music, any music you name. Megan never realised this; it took a while for this to sink in. To highlight the point, I put Auld Lang Syne on, followed by classical music and 80's/90's anthems. It doesn't have to have a beat. We can stretch or contract the moves to match the essence of it. Once she cottoned on to what I was showing her, she connected her phone up and let us rip to her tunes. This pushed her dance passion to the limit. She introduced me to songs that I gladly added to my library. More songs that gee you up making you want to get up from your seat and dance.

It was a little rude to the DJ playing music on our headphones. However. She is young and wants to unleash that exuberance. It was a bit weird seeing us dance completely incongruously to the sound in the room. We were the first to get going and the last to finish. I suspect we spent more than double the time dancing than the rest. Their songs three minutes long, mine six. Six minutes is a nightmare for many a leader. But I can do my bit then hand the baton over to Megan half-way through. Sharing is caring. Sharing is sweet. A longer song can build then erupt and gradually unwind.

My legs ached quite a bit, for we moved a lot with not a lot of sitting down breaks. Over the next few weeks, I found this became a non-issue. I can feel myself becoming stronger, able to walk with more power in my lower body. You get a lot of exercise in Jive without really being totally conscious of it. She wants to do as much as we can before we are locked down again. Time is limited. Time is a pest. We book every night until the doom of doom falls and splits us apart. I lost Laura as a dance buddy in the first lockdown and now I am to lose Megan in the second. Whilst I had manged to recommence talking with Laura, I wasn't quite back to where I was before. The tension had at least drained off a lot though.

Megan was adamant that she wasn't going to see anyone during the month-long lockdown. I had made a suggestion that we could dance in the woodlands-with-a-view. "I have issues", hyper meekly squeakily uttered she as she backed slowly to her car. "No problem, no worries." Probably not a great choice of location. She knows me but not sufficiently well. She sent me some tracks to listen to. My music taste is a bit autistic. I genuinely liked the vast majority of the tracks she put forward. Our music taste aligned quite well. This is unusual for me. I dropped subtle hints about meeting up and having an illegal dance about. To make matters even worse the government decided to mess with our heads. They declared that it might not be a month. It might be 6 weeks or more. Who knows? They are contemptable.

Despair falls and rains down with all the uncertainty. I am then shadow banned on my lockdown protest media channel. No way to vent fury. From tens of thousands watching my trash TV, sometimes several hundred thousand to virtually none. I briefly speculated that maybe the government played a hand in this. Ridiculous, but seems coincidental given the timing. I buy the biggest megaphone available and consider going back out protesting again. I am in my cabin slowly assembling something, sad and dejected. Counting down the days till we can reconvene is not helping. I am at my very lowest point. "Good news, I can dance ...." Oh, my that is very good news indeed. We shall meet in the skate park and dance the afternoons away. I shed a few tears.

Apparently, her mum was meeting with some friends, so she asked why she was therefore not allowed to. The last day before lockdown mark II was incredibly good. I had a double sports day with Malcolm and company, then had a fulfilling glorious evening with Megan. We had danced solid from the moment we arrived till the end of the last song. I also rounded it off with a late entry at the local where Simon was shouting every time he spoke. "Stop shouting Simon", says his horse mad wife. He is not pleased at being put out of business again. We are best of buddies in the anti-lockdown league. They happened to send two of their kids, well they only have two, to Laura's school. It aint cheap.

And there she is waiting on the park bench, her bike chained to it. I feel somewhat honoured. She has come out today to be with me. We get straight to the point, straight into hand to hand non combative dancing. From here on in I have many things on my mind. Many things that I want to do. Many experiments and many thrills. Learning the opposite role is tiring. I can lead effortlessly but both she and I have so many struggles with doing it all the other way around. Nevertheless, progress is swift. We have gone from a pair of monkeys to a pair that can do a basic jockey move smoothly. Piece by piece we add moves. Megan can lead for longer and longer until eventually leading for a whole song. That is an achievement in such a short space of time.

I have a move; Laura's move which I use to hand the lead over to Megan at some point in the song. I also have a shortcut. I simply bring our hands up to her left shoulder, leading her in effect and she instantly smiles and her face glows. She is then off in charge with focus and pleasure. Tongue part out bit between her lips. Concentrating. A ray of realisation befalls my conscious. When a dance was not quite cutting it, when my lead is not quite there, I can hand the lead to Megan and let her have a go. This is useful. This could be a great selling point to the concept of lead sharing. Not only does it address the misogyny, the sexism but it gives men something. It can get them off the hook, on occasions. If you are struggling - let your partner see what they can do.

Lead sharing is a powerful concept. I tell you why. Megan didn't have to spend months learning to lead to make use of it. I would hand the lead to her and if I sensed her drying up, I would take over again. No problem. In the beginning a lady can learn one move and be a lead sharer. The next week she can add a move, do two moves and hand it back. Over time she can do more and more adding things at her own pace.

Then there is the pinnacle of lead sharing. Lead stealing. This is proper, proper fun. You can sabotage and take over the lead. Obviously, one has to yield. A swift crafty sabotage and you are in command. It is friendly battle where you challenge one another, vying for it and become real play fellows.

An obvious question may arise. Does lead sharing mean men will be dancing with men? That is not quite the point of it. No one bats an eyelid seeing women dance with one another for some reason. I have seen a couple of men 'at it'. Though rather rare to witness. Whilst I will mention later that a few fellas did join in with an arm link spin about, more involved dancing with other men it is not something that I relish. I do recall one follower seemed a little more masculine than most other women. We enter a realm of heated, complex, involved debate. I think people will declare themselves, by their own free choice as 'leader-first' or 'follower-first'.

There are some practical issues. Height being one of them. Statistically I would imagine men are taller than women. Many moves have a return on the end – turning the lady back the other way. In some cases you will be trying to get your arm high enough to reach over the top of what is in effect a lamppost. All is not lost. For those in that situation you can pare down the moves and mirror others. You can also push spin rather than return. As most will be leading for half the song only, you can soon figure out enough to get you through.

Not all women will be jumping at the bit to have a go at lead sharing. That is fine. The men will hand over the lead to them and give them a choice. Do a bit of leading or pass it straight back. They get the opportunity at least. This is not something that is to be forced on people. No coercion, just a hope that people will enjoy it.

At the end of a dance one can perform a stylish lean or a cool drop. A flashy finale. I tried one such thing whereby I drop on to one knee and invite young Megan to sit on my knee and then lean over. Megan skipped physics at school along with chemistry. Not biology though. Lean to the left, not lean back Megan. We tumble in front of a fair number that were resting, watching us. I try to shield her head, but it all happens too fast. Chuckle chuckle chuckle went those amused by this foray into showing off. That was in a dance hall on a wooden floor. It is best to avoid executing these antics on concrete, but we have some grass to try some balances. I have someone climbing on me. This is a good sign. Like a real gibbon, Megan attempts to hook her leg behind mine so that we can both lean back supporting one another. Torsion, twisting, bedevils us. There is a slight improvement when one of us stands the other way around. This will take more work.

Facing one another with feet in line we can lean back fine. It is not quite as easy as it sounds. Leaning right back we can tilt our heads and gaze skywards. In awe of the scattered silver spots of rain I press a couple of places on her wrist. She signals the same back. Little things. Little gimmicks. Little joys that bond and tie one another together. Plastic bags to protect the headphones and we dance in the wet utilising the bowls and ramps of the skateboard park. It becomes an adventure. Every two to three days for a month. I leave her there as her father is picking her up. This age gap is not a bother, but it exists. It is all plutonic anyway. I never hug as a greeting nor as a farewell-until-next-time. It is not what I do - but what I don't do.

The moves in my arsenal get expanded. I look up some and invent a few. We practice and perfect many dips and drops. She excels at putting the finishing touches to what I suggest. It feels like a collaboration. I teach her collision avoidance and instil the understanding of its importance. I was quite serious about it. I could fling Megan at speed in many directions aware of the proximity of others, yanking her back occasionally, well before any bump. She pulled me back in time, many times too. Lots of elements come together. However, I want to see her grooving. I want to see her come alive through body shapeshifting. It is not just about learning the moves for me. I want to see style. It will take time. I have patience. It was quite a long time later that I began to see her show me a little of what I wished for.

I poke her left shoulder with my index finger, retreat, then place my hand on her shoulder. She uses her right hand for safety over mine and I swoosh her down and across my body. A nice lean. Many things Megan takes in her stride. I found it quite disconcerting when performed the other way round, her doing it to me. Akin to being put into the dentist's chair and a natural reticence. There is lots to cover. Many permutations with just two arms and two legs each. Hundreds.

Each meet up begun with me enthusing about what we can do in the session. New song. New move. New idea to try. Meeting up at 'the van thing' regularly got me through this lockdown. It proved that lead sharing was a thing. A great thing. We would have a dance, maybe two or three in a row then sit and talk whilst watching the skate boarders and scooter riders fall over. They seemed to fall over, or fall off, 99% of the time they tried anything. Some of them came over to us and said they "didn't mind us being there because we were doing something", unlike the parents that let their dwarfs roam about in the way of speeding riders. The police turned up the one day and asked everyone to go home. None did.

As I said before, Megan's vocabulary is a bit like one of those modern rooms that have a sofa, tv and not much else in it. Minimalistic. However, with the words she does have at her disposal she uses very well. Equally important is her consistent ability to listen. We have conversation. Proper conversation. This is a breath of fresh air. I admit that I did sometimes keep quiet on purpose a few times. A pleasant silence for a brief ten, twenty seconds or so to let her gather her thoughts. Then she would say something. This is all good. I can't believe my luck. I have a fantastic dancer at my disposal and one that I can talk with. Really talk with. She is open. Very open.

Zen ladies and gentlemen. This is a massive departure from standard Jive. It can be a hit and miss affair. Usually a hit. I raise it with Megan, "you can stop at any time, if you feel uncomfortable". "I might not like it?", "I don't know, let's see". I stand behind her. I have selected a well-known slow techno track by Robert Miles. Heavy main electronic beat with a decent melody. Slow. I move her hands about in pseudo random ways. I notice her wrists. The first element that I spot that stood out as most alluring. We are in close hold with the music influencing my movements. Then I stop. I pause and wait. I expect her to take over. I had to lift the cup of her headphone and yell, "your go". We graced through the whole eight minutes of the song.

I slowly edged Megan towards a patch where the sun heated our faces. This zen progressed. She would generate more and more input. Sometimes one of us doing one hand the other doing the other. A shyness returned at one evening in the halls and we deferred until we were in private high up overlooking a large pond. It can be a good thing to wind down before a burst of energy sends the evening off to a nice end. There are no rules, no real structure. Copying what others do is not in the spirit of it. You find your own ownership of it.

It would be quite entertaining to make Megan move to a wand in my hand. One thought leads to another. A remote-controlled Megan. I have plenty of remote controls in my house but also an app on my phone. A piano app and a hip-hop trance dance beat thing too. Some performance art begins. Megan is looking a bit shifty and self-conscious. Left arm moves to the higher notes and the right arm to the lower bank. I stop. I pretend to repair Megan-robot by pulling a trail of innards out of her tummy and finding the fault. Bunching it all back up and shoving it inside with a slam of the door and off she goes to a rhythm. Disco nightclub dancing ilk. I can have some amusement with different changes in tempo and drum sections. "You didn't die", "I did it" she shouts far too loudly, making me feel like I have some newly escaped loon from a Tourette's study department with me. I didn't die either when I tried it the other way round some days later. It is quite a grim thing. Not fun at all. Not for the person doing the dancing anyway. People will find that out too when they brave it in front of a crowd of onlookers in a dance hall one day. Standing on a chair.

A few weeks after these nine skate park afternoons and a few dance nights, I keep going through the sequence of events. Over and over, I go through it trying to look back to a point where I knew. I suppose there was no definitive point. I am sure that on the day her mother arrived to get the car keys it was all straight. I could see the bond she has with her mother. The mother had that motion, that guilty worry that she may have that virus thing running through her veins. She had undergone an earbud injection negative/positive test. Was I worried? Not about that I can assure you. Just trying to convey that this is all dancing and nothing more. It was I can assure you.

Megan had closed her eyes when I shifted into a slow careful dance. Then my turn. One of you needs to have their eyes open of course to avoid going through any plate glass doors or bashing into a fellow groover. It is an odd thing. Having someone there in body but not in sight. I saw her presence as a dark featureless silhouette. Both leading and following is bountiful. It is not difficult, though you will have the arms flailing at times. Megan's compassion was telling when I opened my eyes at the end. She was there for me. The headphones obscure that other thing that you normally attune to too. You have even less sensory idea of where someone is. It is not needed though. We led and followed with our eyes closed.

The headphones are more than a novelty. They enabled us to take the dancing to any place with a flat surface. It enabled an atmosphere to build. They let us be in our own little world of fine music and great company. They do however give rise to some isolation. I have a wooden dance floor at my house and would put the music on loud using the hi-fi instead. Here our heads could connect, that was more sublime. Pros and cons with everything.

We had intended to play a round of mini-golf and have a dance about. It was cold, freezing cold. Damp drizzle horribleness so I suggested, tentatively, whether she would come to my house. She was now fine about it. A big change from a few weeks back. Jolly, jolly good. I didn't want to push it. It is a difficult position to be in, all round.

Lead sharing was bearing fruit. Repetitiveness is kept at bay. It is taxing and exhausting at first, but we began to fall into a neat pattern and could select so many more options now. I had considered making the follow somewhat more masculine. As it stood, I was not too bothered about expressing a smidgeon of femininity. Perhaps the lady leader could strut more and emulate the stag role if she so chose to. There tends to be a lot more turning involved in the follow. That is fine. You can turn in many ways and just go with it. Close holds. Zen. A dance bonding. A connection was beginning to establish itself.

Was she thinking what I was thinking? No don't be daft. I said that to myself more than once. I twisted my hat sideways then went in close face to face. I rubbed noses to see what the reaction would be. She smiled and laughed a little. She *is* thinking what I am thinking. I can't do anything though. There is no way I can make a pass at her. That would be far too risky. Half hour later she said she was going on a 'catalogue dating' date. Blood rushed to my head. Disappointment washed in. "Wish me luck", she says as we parted for the afternoon. I hope it goes really badly I thought. I said nothing. Worse still a week later she was going to see this person a second time. Even worse still, it may have been because of something I had said about the necessity of having to give people a good chance. I have a big problem. For me it is pretty big. The absolute last thing I want to do is draw this dancing partnership to an end prematurely. We have more lockdowns on the horizon. More painful restrictions and I have no plan B. No alternate. No other person that I can link up with. Laura is miles away. Half an hour drive and twenty conversations away from being close to that.

Helen is on and off with Denver, as dance partners, so not an option. I did have Helen around my house a couple of times for first rate dance abouts. She can get into quite a sprint and has it in so many ways. Helen has lots of uses too, lots of tips. She has a wide experience of different dance genres. I feel a bit bad about Helen, she has been so good, good at talking as well. Maybe a bit too good sometimes.

Laura thought that I had accused her of playing games. No Laura, playing hard to get, not playing games. It is an easy mistake, but I did feel like asking how does one get to be a teacher if they can't read? I had established that it was a multitude of grievances. I think the biggest of them all, was the 'discovery' that I had written a few pages in her honour in the book, Ignorance Paradox. Recently discovered said she. That is fair. She had that proof copy some five months back. I had folded the pages in so that she could discover it quickly. I had told her it was her contribution to philosophy. I had made a reference to it in the letter sent along with the coin. It was recently looked at having lain haplessly like a landmine somewhere in a dark corner of her house. Many things stand out for me. Had I not mentioned the clay model - the mother can't avoid being selfish concept or not added that joke to a message, I might be dancing with Laura rather than Megan. Might. Each time I went to the skate park I addressed the notion, 'would I choose Megan or Laura now?' Laura is fanciable. Laura has grace. Laura is quite something. Megan is quite different. I never had any real say in the matter.

I wake up one morning and lying there looking out at the trees. I am now sure beyond sure. Megan is more me. I would choose Megan. No doubt about it.

I do have a raft of psychology tricks at my disposal. I haven't needed to use any on Megan yet. To recap we have Megan as a 22-year-old and Laura as a 36-year-old. That is irrelevant. I never saw Megan as an age, as such, I just saw her as Megan. It was all the grown-up conversations that we had that made one forget how young she was. One is outwardly stunning in my eyes. The other has layers of attractiveness and is vivacious. To be fair I looked hard at Megan's face when spinning very fast, she is more than alright. I need to prove that we can turn 30 times in forty-five seconds. Hand in hand with the background a total blur. I pull in and she giggles at the acceleration. Conservation of angular momentum. If she stops lopping her hair off, I would be fascinated to see what she looks like if it were a lot longer. It is not important, just intriguing. She has an impressive frame and quaint attributes. I would never confess to properly fancying her at this stage, yet I am drawn to her for sure. Wildly so. She is a confetto of fun. She would transform my life and always fulfil me. I would be eternally content. I think I just dismissed her and not paid her that much attention because of her age. I had put Laura on a pedestal and was too orientated towards making progress with her. I had of course known Laura a lot longer.

She is walking towards the main road to get her ride home. As I pass, I wind the window down. "If you are bored on Thursday, perhaps we could go bowling?" She nods, "yes absolutely", meaning nope. 100 yards down the road I am saying to myself, what an earth am I thinking? However. Seeds. Plus, some messages.

The first kiss will never be forgotten. In the car outside her house after she has begun to trust me enough to drop her home. It was the stationary aspect that stood out. Mouth to mouth with no movement, for a long moment. Then so on for a brief while. This could be the beginning of something. However, it will be a protracted beginning. We had danced prior on the dance floor that stood in front of the bowling alley lanes. Obviously not normally considered a dance floor, but just as smooth and as we were the only customers in that night, perfect. One feature I keep mentioning is the time when we are with one another. Time went quickly, every time.

We had sat outside the venue for a good hour or so on a hard-numb-bum inducing bench. We both had something to say to each other but were equally shy. We lay our cards out on the table as it were, and she reached over for my hand and toyed with it. I had nervousness, apprehension but an overriding sense of peace. We chatted, she leant on me. There were many more intense moments to follow in the weeks ahead. There was certainly nothing illegal, nothing immoral or unethical about it. It had been a while, decades since something felt this right, this genial.

Change, novelty, something new, something different is employed to whirl the hours away before the night draws to a close. We have Tango moves, Salsa moves and a range of experimental things to adjust thereby making the restriction of having just one partner all night no less fun than mixing with twenty. We rarely stop for long chats. We had lots to say to each other when we went back to my workshop cabin. She got her hands mucky on the pottery wheel. A fair attempt as midnight rolled past. She sat on my lap, and it was hard to believe it was real. I could have grabbed the bull by the horn and shifted up a gear. The slowly slowly steady approach has a place, but not here. Regrets, mistakes, and important things that I am always behind the curve on. I only realise in hindsight that every inaction is a wretched mistake.

We visit a restaurant, play half a game of cards then perform a reality check. It is not looking like it will work. She interviewed me. The more she questioned the more I realised that it was not to be. Motility. Expiry dates. Those in favour. Those with more than just reservations. Only her cousin was positive. She did her very best to put our case to her family. Her sister heard what was going on and instantly said "cut all ties". Nice. Thanks. Thankfully, Megan said, "No way".

More dance nights are on the calendar plus an extra afternoon out. A live band. The plastic hard floor outside the tent enables us to keep warm via Jive and nowt beats close hold set pieces. It was a wonderful day out. Jolene, Jolene, Jolene, Jolene. My happiness depends on you. I cherry-pick the lyrics here. It was nevertheless sung with passion thereby cajoling us to showcase what we can do together. She looked the part in a classic red dress, and I invited her to bop with gusto. I think this was the first time we truly entered the arena of dance seduction in public.

We had some good topics to go over on the journey there but a less welcome one, from my point of view, on the way back. I was suspicious. Megan was rather 'keen' to get back to the car and made her way to the carpark without any deviation. Certainly no saunter around the city. She has pretty much decided that this was it. Ten days of hope and expectation, now crash and burn with no fireworks to always remember. She had the pleasantness to have a last cuddle. Here I hold a person that I could travel to the roots of dancing styles with. Argentina, Cuba, Spain and many other places are in the offing. Just not with Megan.

We had talked about dancing in Havana. I passed many houses that seemed to have a free for all, booming music and Latin dancing half in the house and half in the street. It would also have been nice to return to Jamaica. They look at our bass boxes and think they are the tweeters. I just kept my backside pushed out and with that can appear somewhat in tune to the way they dance. We agreed that we would dance in the airport, on the concourse and in any fine place along the way. I had some reticence about flying. I became a little travel weary until I made the decision to stick to business class. A twelve-hour flight can seem too short sometimes. Quaffing the ultimate in red wine and tucked up fast asleep in the bed, landing shortly after a heady breakfast. Megan likes to pay her way and could have stumped up the dosh for a splendid trip in one of the best countries in the world. The UK. We would take it in turns to choose where to go. No matter, the excitements of concerts, the thrill of grand vistas can wait. I believe Megan would have got it, understood it, appreciated it far more than many that I have been away with. She interacts with the environment more than the average Joe.

You couldn't fault her for her utmost sensitivity and decency. I was deeply cut up and couldn't help showing it. I told her she *was* beautiful and pointed out to her that I hadn't said that before, on purpose. She appreciated the compliment, the honesty and reason for withholding the acknowledgement. We were there for a long while. Eventually, I got out the car and walked home resisting the urge to look back. Sad but I had buckets of respect and thanks. I have shed no more tears since, maybe enough that evening for a lifetime.

Relief can wash over you after dumping someone in the early stages of dating. I have felt that a couple of times. I said as much to her during the class that followed. She showed some dismay and refuted that. I got the headphones out and we danced voraciously to a drummer's soliloquy in Michael Jackson's band. We used the entire length of the hall. It had become vacated; most had gone home. Our dance spirit is still there. We linked our smallest fingers together outside and agreed to be friends come what May. My word is my bond, and this is something I need not spend ages considering.

Some like someone that really shifts the needle when they stand on the scales. I have identified a key difference between those that have, and those that have a lot less in life. Regarding weight that is. Size matters. It is all according to your personal preference built into you. The difference comes down to one word. An 'a' word. I posed this to people on my video channel. I asked what does a thin (normal sized) person have that a large person doesn't? "Food in the fridge" suggested one. No, I will go with agility. I am fat averse. Not good. Unfair and not equalitarian. I don't treat people particularly different based on how much space they occupy but will date accordingly. I am simply honest about it. Holding Megan was especially pleasant because of her unswerving agility. It feels so different to me. Less is more. Much more for me.

We are invited to be 'body positive'. Except I can't see any positives in diabetes, an earlier death, more chance of being hospitalised and consuming more jet fuel shipping these people about. At least a third of all admissions with complications from this virus was attributable to obesity. How is that a positive message to send out? I was put under house arrest and stopped from dancing because large unhealthy people needed protecting. I have danced with many sizable sorts, and they were amazing, no doubt about that. I want them to dance for longer. More died in the first year of lockdowns from obesity than the virus. People think it best to keep quiet on the matter and not upset the apple cart. Along with woke, overzealous group think, safe spaces and insidious political correctness. It can go far too far. Fat shaming can work and can fail making it a whole lot worse. I believe life is about balance and moderation and it seems out of kilter. Scorn me at your pleasure.

Megan had had a lot to navigate. No more. Boundaries have been imposed. No more kissing. Oh well. It is such a pity. After the last song of the evening, she would rummage through her bag to bring out a small tin of Vaseline. You knew you were in for an embrace. Lips ready to go. Oh well is something I found myself saying quite often. It is a dreary repetitive feature of these date dances, the dance interactions. The snakes and ladders of the romance game. I had rolled so many dice moving things in a direction that adds to the experience of dancing. In years gone by it was always, dancing is dancing. Megan has shown me that having a dancer at home all the time is very appealing.

It is Christmas day. I am in the bath, and I think about another brilliant dancing concept. We could forge a whole new set of moves. Then it struck me. It could alleviate a lot of the apprehension I had about having sex with someone new. That would be a big thing for me. I know lots have it presented to them on a plate. Right there. But don't act. The only thing stopping them is themselves. The lady wants it to go further. The man does anything but. He does anything to extract himself from the situation. This is despite really wanting to roll with the intimacy. I know for sure this situation works the other way round too with women holding back, not making a move or a key step forward.

The day before; Christmas eve, was magical. We set up the tripod and took a third photo. Us on a bridge. A slippery bridge. Very slippery. In the background a folly built all those years ago to look over the lake. A bundle of mighty odd gardens with charm in abundance. I really like this place. It had taken a lot to get her here. She always wanted to meet in a place she felt comfortable – namely with others around. Now she knew I wasn't a 'mad axe murderer' things were very different. Dancing in various spots with Megan was sublime. She lay on the grass. "Close your eyes." The mind-body mini-experience entails touching in random (non-intimate) places. Feel it. Feel the sensation. Let go of yourself and focus on the sensory aspect alone. Megan and mud are no strangers. She grabs my arm tight as she slips slides down a treacherous bank. Megan is an earthly young lady. With hope. After playing poo sticks in the stream, we dance in the tight spaces and inside the dark cavern. A leaf strip made her, then me jump. Not a snake but sure resembled one initially. A couple of mince pies and with her head in my lap soaking up the winter sun. I hold here the dream, ultra-lightly mapping out the contours of her face with one finger. She has hopes mapped out. I have hopes pencilled in - ones that are too easily erased.

It is funny how songs gain so much more resonance once certain people enter your life. Feelings are expressed in those lyrics and melodies. The way I feel when I'm in your hands. Every aspect of life is better in unison. So much more so when the union has far reaching substance.

Hope. She has a hope that she will grow old with somebody. I see it as a coin flip. 50-50 at best. She could end up as a single parent. She could be singing a song about seeing red. That lying cheating bastard would do the inevitable. Or she could get her wish fulfilled. I had a hope that she could succeed in doing a difficult thing. That difficult thing would be to see the positive in the option open to her. She could turn the negative of being left alone in her late autumn/winter years into a positive and there would be compensation for that.

A quiz show highlights a dilemma in the dating game. Do I open more boxes or stick to what I have been offered? You manage to rule out some low life, low numbers and now have a substantial offer on the table. We want to see if we can get something better. People that you trust are shouting out "gamble". The next offer further down the line is not as good, so you say again, "no deal". You end up in the 1p club.

I have been semi-retired for a good while and couldn't entertain getting with her if I had to work full time. My setting my stall out didn't have any effect. Megan wants certainty or at least the potential of being with someone for a good few years before having children and moving in a steady clear direction. I can see that. Megan's ambition is to be the one, to die first. Whilst there is still some life in her left, I want to be sure that there will be plenty more dancing.

A new set of restrictions sets me in another doom and gloom spiral. One excellent day at my home gave me a huge boost. Now I am to cast thoughts of Megan aside. I need to find a new source of hope. I have to wait. I have to guess for how long. This lockdown languishing is not even funny anymore. The last two dance nights have been cancelled. People have cancelled. People that say they are going to go, ought to go. You have messed me up. Had I known in time I would have offered to pay Matt and Sarah the lost ticket sales money. Anything, even if it was just me Megan and no others there. Anything to avoid staying at home. Alone. Sort of.

I know it must be a thousand times worse for those caught up in the health hazards, health service and true physical pain of their waits. Waiting for knee ops, hip ops and other things that were getting seen to in a timely manner before.

Concentrated deaths psychology. If 35 people die in one coach crash, it makes the headlines. 35 people die each week on the roads, but they are scattered about so we pay no attention to them. We could have kept most virus patients at home with oxygen and support from family and carers. Then the NHS could have carried on pretty much as normal. However, the deaths would have come thick and fast, similar numbers but in a concentrated form. Was hanging it out for the vaccine to arrive a gamble that paid off?

Half that were put on a torrid ventilation machine for days on end died. Lots more died when they were sent home, and many returned to die a few months later. If only they hadn't panicked and called it a pandemic. All would have been relatively fine. I write this at a time when I don't know if I am right, or plain bonkers. I don't have the responsibility. I don't have to face the music. I might be wrong, but not completely wrong as the human toll from locking down was significant.

Let's wind Laura up again. She is so gullible. "You are supposed to wear a mask when you walk through the entrance." Her face drops. John backs me up by agreeing and producing a mask from his pocket. Her face drops some more. I adore those tiny shifts in her all telling little face. That fractional movement and hold to a new facial poise to show she is acknowledging her misbehaving. Love it. I don't say this, but think it, "Have you ever seen me in a mask, Laura?" As it happens, I never wore a mask, not once. I never needed to produce my poxy exemption card. Just an announcement that I am exempt sufficed wherever I went. If I recall correctly, Laura chose a nice black mask to hide behind and not because it hides the dirt better than those budget blue ones that people wore for months on end. Behind Jo is not-mine-dear-Laura. "Is Jo going on Friday?" followed by "What about you (Laura)?" "I am mixing too much and have old parents to worry about." To think that it was Laura that gave me the confidence to run a campaign against the lockdown. It was she that poo-pooed it at the start. Now she is full on bible bashing evangelical lockdown promoting insane. Though it could be classic Laura bullshit once again and not the primary reason. She gave me a glare, a stare. A long one, not unfriendly as such, before reeling off this to all in the vicinity. Laura is a nightmare. However, Megan has pretty much replaced Laura in my thoughts. I still have unfinished business though.

The sculpture has been fired. It sits on my shelf waiting for terracotta Megan to be completed. Megan has her hands raised up high. She is in the starting pose for the hallelujah move. I would signal with index and second finger crossed. Once she has her hands at the zenith, I can then place my hand above. Think of it like the electrical pantograph pole on a dodgem. I then have two options. A single shake of the head and Megan crosses her leg over and turns, hopefully in a non-ungainly fashion akin to that of a ballerina in a jewellery box. A double shake and she turns full 360. With the 180 I can scootch around in style and have another head shake. She lowers her right hand on my signal. We then both take each other's waist and turn in a Spanish fiesta, keeping high contact with the left hands. I have seen people lower the hands one by one. Usually with a silly grin and worse still, run their grubby hands along a good section of the lady's arm in the process. Kind of looks greasy, slimy to me that.

It sounds like I have built a shrine to these ungodly souls. In the house of Megan, I suspect the exact opposite has been carried out. The removal of all reminders utilising the wisdom of the millennial age of how to move on well. As for the detached house of Laura, she is as detached as often as I am with many others. So many people we meet and forget about entirely, bar the odd recollection once every thousand days. I had a go at attaching some hair to micro-Laura using a good portion of a paintbrush. Hair is a devil to do in the doll scale. Terracotta Laura is waiting for the photo shoot. A week later I rip the hair off. This is not Laura. This is an illustration that came about without Laura in mind, years prior to meeting her. Mini Megan will be slaked. The clay reused for a small flowerpot. Don't worry it is not some form of voodoo. Re-using things like those that melt crisp packets together to form trendy blankets.

Laura gave me five indicators signalling the missing element in her life. I want to give her some perspectives. I want conversations with her. She wants nothing from me. Maybe my conversation is unwarranted and not needed. I do hope that is the case.

If I am wrong on this, I will eat my hat. Unlike that politician who vowed to do so if the result in the election were as bad as the exit polls suggested, I will find a way.

Laura is a pest. I am a pest. Megan has connected and disconnected with me like one of those dodgy phone chargers. She brings things to life. Then dampens it all. Repeatedly. Determinedly. She gives me belief then I lose faith. Over and over. In the meantime, I can talk about hypocrisy. John is a wonderful fellow and a key player in this dance organisation. He encouraged Matt and Sarah to get the dances up and running again. So, I owe him a lot. A lot indeed. No dances, no discovery. No finding out that Megan is quite something. Something for me. Something to behold. Someone to hold, close. He spoke, not exactly directly to me, but about how we should all dance with everyone. Not just the young ones presumably. Yet, who did I spot having four dances on the same sunny afternoon with just-still-teen Beth? - more than their own wife. Beth being the one with the real bad bop and hair, long nice hair. If I ever get the chance to de-bop her, I will take that constricting hair band out. It got caught in the button at the end of my shirt and ties down her appearance potential. She must be keen to dance, for who dances all night with just one person unreluctantly? All night with her dad. Four or five sessions with Beth and my egotistic self will transform her into a spectacle. Then I would put her in the hands of someone her own age and we have a catamaran on the high seas. She can re-bop when it suits rather than do nothing bar bop.

I have had many fine experiences. I had a pilot's licence and have flown a plane, looping the loop. Egg shaped rather than in a nice circle, but I managed it. I have ambled around the globe and spent a few days in the Democratic People's Republic of Korea. I seemed more drawn to that than the south portion. Rainforests, Red Sea, Dead Sea, so many things to see. Pyramids, temples, catacombs, the top of the pope's house. I have made many connections, but this one with Megan was most meaningful. For me. It was a big deal. Many have had casual dalliances, lots of them. I wanted one with someone that has significance to me. A dream fulfilled.

I just can't do it. I want to. I need to, else I will be in a rut forever. This issue has plagued me since school. As soon as it heats up, I back off. I cool it down and escape. I need more time. Megan initiated more whilst we were dancing. I backed off. I wanted to for sure, but just couldn't. I panicked and of all things got the long bow out. We both had a go at firing a few arrows as far as we could in my field. How crazy. Most certainly not cupid arrows. Megan suggests that I did the right thing for it will save emotional turmoil and prevent me from getting frustrated in the weeks that follow. I don't see it that way. I am frustrated right here, right now and know this will set me back. It will reinforce the idea in my head that I won't be capable of taking it to another stage. Ever. With anyone else.

Finding a dancer to bond with seemed like a new solution. I had never looked for a partner in the dance realm before. That solution is at hand but disappearing out of reach. However, the plan to be brave and forthright works. Step by step. Each day together brings a life changing result. I thank Megan. I thank her, not for taking part but for enabling me to break the curse. Don't be fooled, her face spoke volumes. She was away with the pixies in delight. This won't side-track us from the dancing forever more. There is plenty more mileage in that. We have a full row of sweet jars to dip our hands in now.

I would absolutely love to have a go at my new dancing idea. So many more moves. A whole set of possibilities that lead sharing has a place in. Along with the mirror moves, the fast-slow and all other things that have been improving. I pick Megan up before midday and merrily put the idea across to her. "I tell you what would be really good, Megan, dancing sans clothing." Her immediate reaction, "Well you will have to find a nice lady, to do that with then". "I have one", think I.

I have put an idea out there and made it sound most good. And it was. An unforgettable night made the hangover from three mini bottles of gin drunk neat worthwhile. Megan was driving, so on good behaviour and not drinking. I only saw her mildly tipsy once, on an evening out.

The cabin is big and cosy. Now I know why I spent so long building it. Two weeks laying the floor was time well spent too. Good music on. An ancient hi-fi fed by modern jukebox app on a phone. An all-important, crucial, non-improvable mind-body-soul Megan. It is the pinnacle of happiness. This is our Monday night class. A lesson on being thankful. Being grateful. On this night I know I am lucky. I am most fortunate. I held my nerve. I was patient.

At this stage, in this new arena, I did not do what I usually do. Namely ponder and work out moves to do. I will do them on the fly. I have invention. I am good at creating new variations. My move vocabulary needs brand new words. One need not titillate. Play with of course. Have a go with your partner and see what manifests itself. Consider beginning with dancing like you normally would. I shall explore all manner of options and you need no advice nor permission to do something in a similar vein. We are obviously not the first to embroil themselves in these antics. Possibly the first lead-sharing.

I believe that the reason it works is because of my age, not despite it. Though I did think that about Laura too. Laura is not on my mind now at all. I still owe her. I always will. Megan and I know we have a connection. Connected by dance at first but by many other valuable things as well. Age brings wrinkles. Less hair, and one or two white stands. I am semi-confident that this escapade would have been less likely with Laura. Or to be blunt, beyond improbable. Thus, not bubbling with Laura is fortuitous.

Having had my few minutes of fact finding with Laura, my compact Megan came over to me. She had finished a catch up with some others. We greeted each other like we always do, eagerly – a bit like university students, proper warmly. Laura tutted, fractionally put out, so bounced over to John and garbled some trite about her work to him. Little things. I love them.

I am able to pause. To think before reacting. I am able to make considered responses. In my youth I would have batted the ball back too quickly. I am 'dating' a 23-year-old. A wise and clever one. Tactful and not easily led. As such. I have to utilise any advantage I have, not to take advantage but to make it have maximum effect. I am a little cunning. I am, however, no con man. If she accepts my offer of 'marriage', I sincerely mean it, genuinely.

I said I was dating a 23-year-old, but this twenty-three-year-old and I have agreed that this is a more see how it goes affair. An affair that is not an affair, not having intimacy with two people at the same time sort of thing. I had given up talking about the merits of anything long-term. I read something months later that basically stated that not much good ever comes from discussing a relationship. Better to just live it. This needs more thought. However, it tends to bubble up from time to time. Am I secretly hoping that it could be something permanent? In truth losing interaction with Megan is not palatable. I am invariably positive, we both were each time we engaged with one another.

There is another positive. You know when you sit there thinking about things, problems, issues, well it turned out that we both pondering about precisely the same things, problems, and issues.

Do you like puzzles? Megan is not enamoured by them. Self firmbond 1000000-14, 'twas sent to her via text. We did a fair amount of talking by text. She would raise random topics. Intrigues of language, socio-political items and of course feminism. This is interesting to me. I do notice however that she is a bit scatter headed. One line of a poem I sent months later drew attention to this. Finish what you start. She seems to start lots of things. I wanted another word for 'lover' so looked up a synonym on google. Inamorata was an option. A good one as it turned out:

noun
1. **a person's female lover.**
   "His new inamorata is a twenty-two-year-old mannequin named Jennifer"

When she hit 23, we turned up at the dance hall and 23 was 'shouted' out, pointed out, loudly by John and company. Snide indirect disapproval was evident for sure. Megan found Helen's "you two make a lovely couple", a little irksome. Megan declared many times that she was not in the least bit bothered by what people thought about the slight age gap thing.

I bought her a pair of antique earrings containing a trio of crystal-clear fine diamonds. Some things just speak to you. These had a symbolic sentiment. With them in place I felt that I had modified her in a teeny-weeny way. This is the soul of getting with someone, it expands your sense of worth, gives you meaning and purpose. People connecting forms something. It is far greater, for me, than the two solitary individual components.

Nothing puts me off Megan. Maybe some things will irritate each other later down the line, but so far so good. Many will stop courting someone when something they find 'icky' comes to light. It is not that

I am simply being tolerant. Neither is it me looking at things overall, but cherishing aspects of an other. Now that I can't go to the pub, all sports are off, I can't visit a shop, Megan is more than a mere blessing. She is the difference between living and existing. Thoroughly living. Not biding time, not consuming a life in hope.

We are drawn to take a look at what is over on the other side of the road. To listen to the pack of crows. There is the crunch of the frozen grass beneath our feet. The twilight fans through the trees. An orange cinema film projector effect. We got to the far end of the field and had a moment together. My arms around her standing behind and observing the extremely misty day. I mention this for with Megan life is richer. Ten minutes waiting for the car tyres to be fitted without the huffing and puffing that I usually have to bear. This was the day the relationship was fully consummated. I had hoped it would that day. I know she was most keen too as she was dismayed when I said I had to go get the car sorted before the garage shut. Her spirits lifted when I said that we have a good hour before we need to go.

Evenings together flew by. Days out blurred into an un-jarring smooth moment. Having Megan to mess with was productive. In the days between meetups, I conjure up more dance variety to use next time. Mirroring is one of the many things that showed how possibilities can be expanded. Many moves usually done on the right side with the right hand can be done on the left side with the left hand. This is an ideal way to confuse the hell out of someone that has been on the dancing circuit for a while. Variations folks. Intentional ones. There are times where you end up left hand to left hand and have nothing that usually fits. A mirror move works here.

I have always had a hunch that Megan had it in her. She was wretchedly reserved. Neither of us like being told what to do. I saw some signs emerging of her flourishing moves with some style and panache - though only when the music took hold and never on command. Then it happened. She showed me a bit of her Salsa. The hips moved man. They moved. All I need do is get her to transfer that substance into the Jive flow.

In the meantime, we had a bash at merging some Tango into it. Our ideas came together. We both had an input. We did some steps - square patterns, then practiced the head turns. A sharp clear turn of our heads from eyeballing one another, with her face beaming, to a ninety-degree twist and hammering down the hall. Each twist away then facing each other is synced by me raising our clenched hand grip. A leg wrap enabled us to guide the other in another direction, often necessary to avoid people in the way. A few cones came in handy at the park to get it right first. A little of this before we break back into a Jive routine. So many additions were gradually put into place. There really is no end to what one can do when you let your imagination run riot and have a willing participant.

We spent a while going back to basics towards traditional Jive. Had the bridge not been so slippery we could have used that to make sure we are staying within the invisible tracks. Moves are executed fast and furiously, preferably close to the beat. The lady will move up and down the unseen tracks with the man stepping out of her way. I have seen Debbie's daughter do it with aplomb. Fascinating to watch - the once. Once you have seen it, it is rather dull.

A walk across the fields through woods, up a crooked ladder tied to a tree enabled me to take my last photo of Megan. Top down with her looking up smiling vibrantly and Ruby her dog holding still. We had a little dance to three tracks on a small patch of hardstanding. We needed a drink. We bought some supplies and headed over to a viewpoint. It was cold. She had the cheek to ask if I could see the most distant hills. Any painter knows that the further away a feature is, the less distinct, the lighter the colour it is. I can see it as well as she but have more of a struggle with reading tiny words. Age catches up with you. It is a shift that takes place as starkly as when your balls drop, voice breaks and a first period stains the clothes.

Upon my lap she uttered "I *so* love you", in a way one might say they love a holiday resort. She bounded over from the driver's seat. We kissed quite few times and then for the last time.

Some weeks back she wanted an idea for something to draw. I sent, "Using only two non-complementary colours show fragile balance". She kindly let me have this picture. I framed it and mounted it on a bearing. It is finely balanced. A spider will walk along the top and it tips.

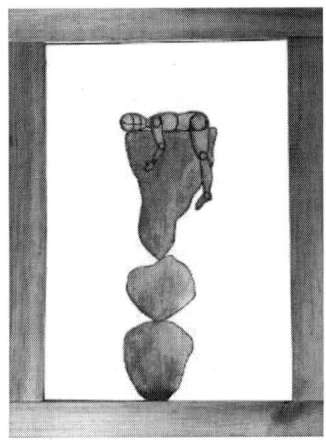

I welled up a little. That is me. One wrong move and it all tumbles down. If I say one thing, do one thing, not do one thing it is all over. I have swerved and dodged all sorts. Many close calls. Many near misses where I refrained from saying something. Even if I manage to avoid numerous pitfalls it is inevitably unsustainable. The age disparity is a stretch. I had made a few observations over the past year. These came in useful. I have a good idea of how to play things. However, it is not a lot of fun being in this position. Sooner or later, I am to get a text message that I dread. To be frank I dreaded most text messages. I knew from the outset that it would be a temporary thing. She would get a boyfriend at some point and that is me done. It lasted far longer than I initially expected. However, when I am finally beginning to relax a little, in it comes.

One introductory word sets the tone of what we are about to read. With Laura it was 'unfortunately'. Unfortunately, the one dance night I would have gone to, I am away. With Mega-14 it was 'hey'. Oh, dear here we go. Hey, how about we leave it for a week or so then reassess. The 'or so' provided the most merriment. A bit like the government and their lockdowns of a month or three or so depending on the weather and other pseudo random variables. No problem I say, we can back pedal if you like. Our Monday night is off I gather. Boy I hate cancellations. The steaming into the supermarket, no mask, no care in the world to get some bites to eat was a risk that needn't have been taken and a waste of anticipation. Was it that? Was it me showing the comments on the videos? She sure looked aghast. I had become immune to the less supportive types. More were in favour on aggregate, but the dissenters stand out. I am after all campaigning against the grain of current thinking. I should have showed her the videos that got nothing but support, land I bought for re-wilding and philosophy hits. She writes, "the police are seriously clamping down. Its knuckling down more". There were many possibilities. Maybe it was a combination of many things.

I am at this point reasonably sure that an assessment has already been carried out. I read between the lines to confirm my suspicions. A 'loooovely' is used widely at the end of a dating session to leave it there and leave me be. A convivial parting pleasantry. So too is the "You can always text me when you need a chat". "What did you get the ariel thing?!", tells me she is never coming over to use it.

I must be a glutton for punishment, but if there are girls involved, I can't resist. They were both agile. One an office worker, the other a hippie. The hippie had tied the ring above a menacing rock. The beach had only one tree available. If you fell off, you were fucked. Doubly fucked as Monserrat hasn't exactly got the sort of A&E that we are used to. Nevertheless, with their encouragement I did get myself up on it. The next day

I had similar sensations reminiscent of those after Zumba. There are muscles we neglect to put through their paces every day. My ring languishes unopened in the packaging it arrived in. Oh well. As with sex, dancing, sports, it is not quite the same on your own.

She might think I am laissez faire but doesn't get it. As far as I am concerned this virus is not a big deal. Yes, some had it bad, I didn't. I drive a big car so that if involved in an accident my chances of survival are better. I don't take unnecessary risks. I spend ten minutes tying ladders with guy ropes and use a harness. A little effort keeps one out of hospital. If I took her to India or China it would be me telling her for the umpteenth time to avoid ingesting any water in the shower and use bottled water to clean her teeth. One thing me and Laura both did unreservedly was hit the loos right away to wash our hands after dancing.

Stay home, stay safe albeit knowing that six thousand perish each year in our not quite as safe as we think homes. Grenfell tower. As I edit this, news comes in from Miami. People sleeping safe and sound in their building when it collapsed. Over one hundred crushed to death, safe from the virus now. My sailing friends, Clare and John were anal about the rules and nonsense. Some people put a mask *and* a visor on. Whilst driving. Maybe they should have too when they were within fractions of a second from being decapitated by a large wodge of tree falling and bouncing on and over their convertible.

After a week of trying to reason with her, I test the waters. Had I been able to see her at the dances like normal times I would have left it, but these are far from normal times. Before I proceed, I need to be sure. I get multiple direct confirmations. "So, no more dancing even if the lockdown is for 3-4 months?",

"Yeah [Sad not-smiley-face-emoji]". A refusal to meet for a coffee even at a social distance. Declining an afternoon using the acrobat ring and a play on the ride-on mower. No getting together even if I obtain a nuclear/chemical/biological protection suit and a toss of the coin to see who would wear it. She insists that when the restrictions are lifted, we can carry on our merry way with the dancing. I am sceptical. I might have got it wrong, but I sensed that she had no intention of ever meeting up again. All that remains is text messaging. I did enjoy learning a good deal about dogs from her. I had always known there were ones of different colour, and some are bigger than others. I tried to guess the breed going from the pictures she sent. Cockapoo? Labradoodle? Etc. "I said pure breeds!"

She sees no long-term future in our 'relationship' so can swipe me aside quickly. As quick as we do on a dating app. Understandable. She claimed that her decisions were not being understood or supported. I think she is right. I am not grasping what she is saying properly. It is over text message, and it is hard. I don't think either of us had any real clue as to what the other one was going on about. We both jumped to the wrong conclusions. So utterly different to what would have gone down face to face. But we can't meet so that was 90% of the problem. When she mentioned that she was thinking about closing her business, I was quite upbeat. More time to meet up. Instead, I proffer up what I would do. Note, I would not close no matter what. She had it set up all safe, sound and tax generating to save lives via the government coffers onwards to the national health service. There is a hundred times more chance her mother would bring the plague into their realm given that over half have managed to in her profession. She wants to alleviate suffering from the virus, and I want to alleviate suffering from the lockdowns. This difference in attitude affects the choices me and Megan make. I want the lowest end death toll. That is the sum of those dying by the virus and by the longer-term consequences of repeated shutdowns.

Exasperation barely covers it. I had avoided supermarkets, filled my tank right up to keep visits to petrol stations to a minimum and barely went out. She was made to feel like a potential murderer if one mistake, one gulp of air, leads to an infection. Kids were forced to go to school and forced to endure the anxiety of being the culprit - a killer in the community.

I found it hard to cope with her decision to stay at home during this new lockdown. She was my quasi-legitimate adult support bubble person. Politicians flouted the rules. We only got to hear about some. Their illicit affairs, meals in large groups, traveling whilst testing positive and so on. But us, we must obey. And suffer.

It felt like there was a dark force in the vicinity. We were having a wonderful time. We both were. We sparkled in each other's company. It was great. Not everyone saw this. I will go as far as saying, spite came into it. Pure spitefulness on the part of those that believe they are doing the right thing for her.

I have always had this overriding notion that people are not supposed to have fun. We ought to be working and keeping our head down. Going out and really enjoying ourselves – that is for errant folk. This just reinforces that feeling.

Megan may have had a better handle on the stubborn realities than me. However, I ask you this, if you were forcibly separated from your partner for four months, would you be a little agitated?

One text message and the light is switched off. The tunnel is dark and long. For months now I will do nothing but suffer the impact of this pernicious human rights abuse. It is illegal to dance with others. Illegal to see my family. I haven't seen my mum and dad in well over a year. Illegal to do the most basic things that we humans have been doing for tens of thousands of years. All these people abiding by guidance thought up on whims and breezy glances at science. It impacts me in a way that sets in motion stupidity, regret and badness. I am forlorn. I express something to Megan that was plain awful. The messages coming my way did not hide the truth. They were becoming more annoying leading up to me blowing all the bridges we had between us. At no point have I ever been angry with Megan. I never will be. Frustrated and helpless at the circumstances, but not one bit angry with her.

I did surmise that I might not be handling rejection too well. Doing anything to avoid it finishing. She was my freedom ticket. I did say to her that I felt like I was putting on her. If you have someone, you care far less about the impositions that society place on you. It was the pubic that pushed the government to take away our liberties. A public that was quite selfish. It was largely alright for them. Many were getting payments and a nice long holiday. The things that made life good for me were all closed up. Megan opened it. If I can see her every few days, all is well. And now of course it is not well. I had a taste of something good. I am now down a flaming well of despair. Maybe I made too much of a big deal about this. Roll back a few years and the lockdown would have been a minor inconvenience. I have had a great experience; I sure am fortunate to have finally seen what is possible. I have though, got to wait and wait and flipping wait till I can see if I can repeat the exercise. As you get older time seems more precious. This theft of time, time we will never get back is lamentable.

As the weeks pass, I know it was a mistake. A big one. It removed all hope. It ended something so special. No apology will do. Texting is fraught with danger. I said something that was easy to misread, misunderstand. No excuse is sufficient. Even if it had the expectation that it would make her rethink the choices she makes in the hunt for a relationship with someone. It makes me wicked and unappreciative. At least it was only saying something. Not doing something bad. Lots do bad things.

I have more remorse inside me for spewing a text message out than those that did dastardly things to her long before we danced together. He didn't feel too bad about what he did. That is known. Nevertheless, it is not the point. My understanding and patience always had a limit. I did well overall. As anyone would. As anyone should.

I made another huge error. I let things go. I should have pulled her up on a couple of things. In my mind I don't want to send more messages. That could make it worse. I should have. She said that I was clearly trying to hurt her feelings by sending a series of nasty texts. That is so wrong. I wanted to apologise for not giving her the same regard as I gave Laura. It took time for me to appreciate how equal she was to Laura, how much better than Laura she was, for me. I really, really, really, was not trying to hurt her feelings. The compliments were real and valid. When she said 'no means no' I ought to have pointed out that, that is generally used only in certain circumstances. It has a connotation that people can get the wrong idea about.

Revenge is a dish best served cold. This is not revenge. I did kind of agree to write Megan out of the story, but it is much less of a story without it. I assumed that she would not write about me either. She decided to pass on messages that I had sent to her after she called the dancing a day. She became a tad aggressive. I simply sent her an orchid as a sign of peace and a thankyou card. Megan told me she was a hot head at times, and she sure is one. Some ex had gone to the trouble of mopping the bathroom floor. Except it wasn't to Megan's exacting standards. Consequently, she flew into a rage and belittled and not beguiled him. Loudly.

I have no grudge against Megan. None whatsoever. I prepared myself for various questions that will come my way when the dancing resumes. I was to simply say this; The dancing was fantastic, she was good, good company and real fun indeed. People will always focus on the tiny bit of negative. Thus, I would be ready for that and respond with, "there are two sides to a coin, though I except it was my fault", and leave it at that. It would take far too long to explain it all.

Two months pass since I ended contact with Megan and we are now not too far away from taking steps, dancing steps again, when I get a call out of the blue. It is Matt. I instantly think, oh good some update on the dance resumption. But no. I am to be excluded from all dance classes and dance events in his franchise. I have been accused, put on trial, and convicted of harassment. All in my absence. This is great. No due process. No calling me to let me know that complaints have been made, assuming there were any. No asking my side of the story. Just a life sentence of barring and stigmatisation. The air of triumph, the gleeful way he made each announcement, each thing I am forbidden to go to, was maybe cathartic for him, but smarting for me.

I try to argue my case, but this is a full-on kangaroo court. He believes it is black and white. My only option is to provide proof that I didn't send various text messages. He will not listen nor countenance any discussion on the matter. No option to appeal either. So, I send an appeal anyway. I call him petulant. I tell him that it is a slur. I tell him that I am acutely aware of what constitutes harassment. I have had to deal with equivalent issues myself. I get all the information, put it to the person accused and get their response. Then make a decision.

In truth my bothered-ness is not huge. I had already resigned myself to the situation. Returning to dance without Megan is not going to be as grand. Roe rather than caviar. I want to move the dance project on, even if that is part of the time. I want to dance with everyone again but need that extra aspect along with it. I would have to arrange a partner of some description for four weeks then maybe, just maybe classes with all again afterwards. It would provide an opportunity to see the pair again and an outside chance that some reconciliation could begin with Megan. I can attempt to be convivial and gradually rebuild something, possibly. I have been excommunicated from all those I have got to know.

I had already sowed some seeds with two candidates and had another two in mind as well. Lottie was a firm favourite. Fit - athletic, nice height and with the general structure that appealed. She also had a stare that reminded me of none other than Laura. I paid the entrance fee as usual and then asked her whether she likes dancing. Not once but three times. No response.

A total blank. The next week I asked four more times and got a partial yes, no and this glare. I said it was Jive, Becky said, "go on Lot .... would do you good". Sadly, she just looked at me and nothing more, "no .... no". Oh dear. I must have an awful chat up line technique. Except this was made clear that it wasn't an asking her out. Maybe another bit of persistence will bear fruit. Not needed now as I am banned.

The other candidate, Emily, was an avid nightclub goer. She had been unable to party on two significant birthdays and was up for dancing again. I told her about the lead sharing concept and enthused about partner dancing. My aim was to pay her a few visits and keep mentioning the dancing. Then ask her if she would like to give it a bash. Only four weeks after all. She was a different kettle of fish compared with Lottie. Easier to talk to for sure. Positive vibes. Anyway. Wasted effort. I did at least make Becky laugh and smile quite a lot.

Am I guilty of harassment or a victim of a witch hunt? My issue is that I have a black mark on my name. The insinuations and accusations are grating. I will tell it the way I see it and you can make your own mind up. It seems odd that Laura would contact Matt seven months after the event. I had visited Laura unannounced, but she had made me a friend on the friend tagging website. It was a little awkward at first, but she soon came around. We chatted for twenty minutes or so whilst she dragged a huge white sack filled with leaves and droppings. I was there in part to ensure that she was alright. Her muddled message saying she was stressed was nonsense. She was not stressed. She was absolutely fine. We talked about all kinds for quite a while. All good. Nothing remarkable, nothing negative, all relaxed and happy. I expected her to mention the book. I had it on hold, but nothing, so took that as a sign of no discontent with it. She had the only copy, no one else saw it. One thing is for sure, I wouldn't be going back uninvited. I had decided that for myself. I had not been back ever. It is all ok. I do understand the concern, there are nutjobs out there that are not being dealt with.

Wind forward a month and I am talking with her for nearly two hours, and we had a dance. She shifted her whole body in my direction, hand on head and this body language is good. Whilst she had not been too impressed at first, she was now fine. Maybe I wore her out a bit.

I gave her space during the strolls class. I spoke to her little by little, and it was soon done and dusted. It was all cordial. Ill feelings had died down completely. We were forced to contact people to link up. There were many that had all kinds of shenanigans. People letting one another down. Arrangements that worked and arrangements that didn't. This was brought about by lockdown. Lockdown or no lockdown we must behave of course but I would never in a thousand years have contacted Laura if there was no lockdown. Period.

I had sent the letter to say goodbye. As far as most of us were concerned the dancing was over. The club set to disband and that was it. For me it was done with Laura. However, it wasn't over. It did return. So then it was game on again.

There would have been no tiff with Megan either if it were not for the strain of being tied down to your house for months on end. It a double-edged sword as I concede that the lockdown did provide the opportunity to spend lots of time with one person. Not great for many as I heard many grumbles, but for me at this stage it was perfect.

I was then accused of following people, what the f. Not stalking Matt conceded, but following people online. What utter slanderous nonsense. What people? Why on earth would I follow people online? What is the point? What next is he going to claim? I murdered those million people in Rwanda? I caused the defect in Apollo 13? This is like cancel culture. People's lives are cancelled by rumours and hearsay. No investigation, just information brought to someone's attention that is not verified or put to the person accused. No opportunity to refute the claims. Karma and 'what goes around comes around' springs to mind.

Anyone who runs a business will relate to problems that pop up that are not exactly what we initially signed up for. Organising, tax affairs, websites, security issues and countless things that have nothing to do with the core of the business. In this case, Matt set out to teach but then he finds himself dealing with all the problems that the public bring with them. It is all supposed to be fun and a great learning experience, a dance learning experience, but ends up being a fraught, contentious nightmare at times. Do you jump on it early, let it go or make a stand when you think enough is enough? Who knows what is best?

We can make a mountain out of a molehill; it is just a dance class and some evenings where people have a get together. The same issues arise when children are taken into care due to perceived wrong doings by their parents. Vast numbers of families are torn apart when people come to the wrong conclusions. Cognitive bias, people seeing things that confirm unfounded suspicions. The damage is horrendous – some parents get close to suicidal and scarred for life. Highly qualified people making poor assessments when they have been told that an injury is believed to exist. Out of excess caution babies are removed for months from their families.

Fair game my friends. I knew Laura was going to the pub, it is a dance night. That is fair game - to show up. Had I scrutinized her activities and discovered she is going to a clown costume convention and 'just happened to be there', and 'bumped into her', that is not fair game. Anyone doing that is spying on someone's activities and passively stalking someone. I only browsed her photo/info archive the once. There was one standout comment that said a lot. Apart from a few pictures, the main point of interest was seeing her age in black and white.

It wasn't just that that stabbed my pride, but his comments re, "from a human perspective", that are simply unfair. He reckoned I should re-evaluate my dealings with women. If that is the case, then heaven help the vast majority of men (and women) in this country. Besides, there are other attendees that have done a lot worse things than me. By far. I know I pushed the boundaries, I did wrong to some degree, but he made me feel pure evil.

Perhaps he is right. In the quarter of a century since I have been on the dating scene everything has changed. The rules are now totally different. However, I would never in a month of Sundays corner someone and block their path like Phil. I would never dream of running after someone and slapping them around their face like Dean - just because they walked away from them.

He said, "I have seen you at it". Namely he has seen me hassle Megan presumably. I was outside with her for a while, yes, but harassing her? Quite the opposite. It was delicate and I know, I have seen it, I have witnessed what being pushy is. I could swear. One could get verbally abusive towards those that witness situations like this and read it wrong. They think they understand what is going on, but they don't know the half of it. Full story. And he could have got the full story if only he cared enough to obtain it. It was jolly unreasonable of him.

I tell you; I gladly found the resolve to be sensitive, diplomatic, and fully understanding with Megan. I was careful and patient. I had to tiptoe about in certain quarters. That is nothing to rave about. Lots would do the same. Being kind to being accused of the kind that is harassing is objectionable. It is a smear. Not once did I or she for that matter, ever presume anything. All things we did was done after talking about it first. All things.

I walk into a pub and look this way and that, then this way and that. I am then pounced on by a lady who is there celebrating her husband's retirement from the police force. "I don't think you like social occasions", she glibly gets me wrong entirely. I am looking to see where that piece of flotsam, Mark is. He has been getting ever more brazen and revolting. If my partner is alone or with me, he is still trying it on. I do like social occasions. Very much so and am not, as she intonated, some kind of introvert shy, retiring sort. A full psychological analysis of me is being carried out, step by step by her. All these vulgar amateur 'psychologists' including Matt make the same stupid mistake. They come to conclusions based on one piece of evidence. Two pieces gives you a 50/50 shot at being right. Three and you can put money on it. Many jumped to the conclusion that Megan may be a lesbian based on one thing, her presentation. I didn't. One thing is not enough to draw any conclusions. I didn't care one iota anyway. The theory regarding Laura's predicament; five items make it bankable.

The "I don't know your situation", was more code for, "I am not bothered what situation you are in". As far as he was concerned, I had breached his code of conduct. Fair enough. I pointed out that most of the dancing with Megan was not in his halls. I met her there though, so that gives him cart blanch to nose deeply into our affairs. Aside from that, I feel very fractionally bullied out.

It does also say, "We will not discriminate according to sex, gender expression or sexual orientation ....". But you do Matt. You make the women line up in front of the men and assume they will follow.

My parents met at a dance. It was the in thing and a very common way to meet people. My father went away for a year in the merchant navy. My mother was prepared to wait a year but gave him an ultimatum on his return. He had suggested another year away. Evidently, he chose to find another job and settle down with her. I didn't have the patience to bide my time for four months let alone a year. I behaved like a teenager that always expects to get their way.

With a long history of people coupling up, showing off, impressing, validating and fighting, dancing can be fractious. With testosterone running high and people wishing to save face, it is not difficult to see why some say all is fair in love and war. Nowadays, people understand that partner dancing is no longer primarily about pulling.

I have been known for my flippancy. I do recall my teacher wrote on my school report that my flippancy had improved. I said something simply because I do not want to hear that something horrible has happened again. I thanked her first for everything. I was truly grateful. Then I suggested that in the same way I changed who I mixed with to improve my business prospects, maybe she could gain from changing who she dates. If you fish in a swamp, you pull out a crocodile.

I am somewhat put out that everything I did which I see as kind and caring is used against me. Trying to make amends makes me a bad person. Trying to apologise gets misunderstood and used against me. I am punished for trying to sort it out. Punishment, punishment, and more punishment. What makes it feel far worse is that those that did awful things get nothing at all. They move on to the next victim.

I know what it is like to be held down. At the mercy of someone else. This can be the pivotal factor that make sexual attacks so abhorrent. I know others, men and women, that have been subjected to this and I understand the long-term impacts. Most are not sexual in nature but still deliver memories that don't fade fast.

Karen lived with me in a shared house, some students, some nurses. One evening her boyfriend's brother Mick decided to jump on her. He held her down for quite a while. Her boyfriend, John didn't do anything. No reaction. Maybe he felt awkward with it being his brother. He failed. It doesn't matter who is involved, it is not acceptable to watch and do nothing when someone is being held against their will like that.

There is more to this story, and I had hoped to convey the essence of it to Megan. She would not have liked to hear it. However, the knowledge of the way things are, has kept me alive. The knowledge of the way things are, has meant I have not been beaten to a pulp. To put it plainly, there are shitheads out there. A good few of them. They do not care. They act rashly, violently, and instantly.

I adored Karen. She was a lot of fun. She looks out of the window in the middle of the night and sees it is snowing. Downstairs goes she and bundles up some snow. In my room she comes, comes not cums, and plasters me with it. No problem, I will get her back soon enough with some other prank. However, not all take messing about like this so calmly. Karen was winding up Mick quite a bit. He is like a lion in the zoo, prod it and it will lash out. Mick is a shithead. The point is that you may be in the right, but they are always right no matter what. How many are in hospital because they didn't backdown, escape or surrender early?

Me and Kevin had been trying to remove a pesky tree trunk and went back inside for a drink. Carlos and Kevin got into a 'discussion' about a physics related matter. Carlos was right, Kevin was wrong but no, Kevin has an axe in his hand. He is right. How many times have you been a quarter of the way across a road at a pedestrian crossing and realise that the car isn't going to stop for you? You are in the right but could soon be dead right if you don't step back. I am trying to say to Megan, that you can look at who you choose to be alone with. You can gauge better when to get out. You can also change your manner. I am sorry Megan, but maybe I saw things. They increase the potential of trouble. A shithead will take advantage. You can alter things to stay one step ahead. Most men will be fine, but some are shitheads. It happened to you before, I sensed it may happen again. So, I said something that was supposed to get her attention. It pissed her off. I am not sorry. Had it worked it would have been for the good. I have been to thousands more bars, clubs, discos, you name it, than her and seen it. Once every few years or so there is bother. Bother that could have landed nasty punches on me for being there and not causing it. They are right in that moment, that is the way things are.

Whilst there are dangers and a risk of trouble, nights out are a highlight of life. Miscellaneous groups of people chatting and practicing wit. Getting a round in for someone they just met. Learning and sharing. What words fully convey the electric emotional buzz that pervades the coming together of souls in that moment of time?

Megan was not the same towards me after these few ascii characters were delivered. She asked me not to contact her anymore. "I will not accept being spoken to like this." She was not able to dance for months. I had calculated that in four months' time I would get a "sorry I have a partner now", "so can't dance with you, sadly". Over the years I have seen couples quickly switch from ultra-loving to fisticuffs. From being on the same side to opposition to all they stand for. In this instance I have no ill feeling towards Megan.

Being born male in this country puts you at a huge disadvantage. And it gets worse as each year passes. If a woman were to send a thankyou gift to a man (some chance - highly unlikely) it would be taken for what it is. Appreciation. When a man does so, they are either up to something or after something. I am beginning to think that I have been batting for the wrong team. There is me trying to do something about the inherent sexism in dancing whilst it is the men that are being appallingly maltreated. We have a law that prohibits girls from being circumcised, but no such law would ever be countenanced for boys. They are bundled into a carry cot by their most loving mothers to see a degenerate who slices a piece of their penis off in the name of it looking better and it being cleaner. Why not remove all their teeth while they are at it so that they look better and have less to clean each day? The piece they remove usually grows to the size of one's palm, it is quite a lot. The head becomes less sensitive, and all kinds of issues arise. Some men get flash backs of sorts from the fun the knife man had tying the baby's legs and arms up first to stop them defending themselves. There is a solution. Because society cares far more for women than men, we could look at it from a different angle. Sex for women is generally better with men that have not been mutilated and not had a vital piece stolen from them. I won't bother to explain as nobody is that interested. I could rattle on about who is always last in line for custody of the children and so on but will leave it at that. Megan described her feelings about 'women and children first'. She wants women to be considered as capable as men and need no special dispensation. I agree.

"Boys will be boys", lambasts my father on the news that his grandson has successfully inseminated his girlfriend. A lockdown child. Girls adore satisfying, gratifying, sanctifying sex as much as boys do. Keeping this in mind has helped me with my holding back issue.

Megan welcomed a perspective on the parallel issues men face in the gender wars. She has spoken at length with many women, but not heard a lot from men. I can add one more thing to this. In this culture, people always side with women. Matt spent a while getting information from many sources to back up his perception of events. This sets in stone a one sided, ill informed, biased narrative. His level of effort was well deserved because Megan is female. He spent 0 hours, 0 minutes, and 0 seconds verifying accusations with me, because of course, I am a man. If I had called him to say that Megan was harassing me, he would have just laughed and put the phone down.

The 'multiple sources' is telling.

I sent her some of the story. Unedited scraps to be used for this book. She was reading each snippet but not saying anything. It created a string of texts. Then I stopped. She did ask me several times, "When will I be allowed to read your piece mentioning me?"

Anything I do, or not do, will be transformed into bad. Turdified. Humans have been turning lovely food into brown stuff, since forever. They do the same with nice actions, nice intentions, niceties of all kinds that relate to the newly despised person. I am twisted and toxic. Or what I have done has been twisted into toxic waste. Chucked onto the toxic trash heap with all the others. All men are rapists and assumed so, until we are very certain they just might not be. As most men are nasty, we can assume that all men say nothing but things that are nasty. It is the default assumption. I was trying to apologise. I was providing the truth about my fallibilities. Admitting to my failings. It seems like a long string of texts but copy and paste a paragraph of this and you will see it runs a long way on a mobile phone text message. It wasn't that much I sent. It is an exaggeration. I was trying to convey that I cared and valued what we had. She reckons it is gobbledygook, ludicrous. Oh dear.

Megan thought me sending texts was not the best way for someone to deal with their feelings. That is true enough. I suppose I could be more sub-human. More emotion free. More capable of handling a snap dumping. I said it went from super good to super shit in an instant. It is hard to lose someone without knowing the real reason, especially after it had all been going so well. She thought that I thought she was not being genuine. She may be a crafty little bugger, but she is one of the most genuine people I have met in a good while.

I then leave her be. For a while. I dropped off a copy of a picture of us in a dance pose along with an eye mirror. Only fair she has a copy though she may do what I do with Xmas cards – put them on the fire to see how stingy people are. Some burn real nice, others not much more than a whimper. Eye mirrors are not easy to make. Silver needs to be inset into the brass surround and mounted in a round carved out piece of wood. You hold it up between two fingers and stare into your own pupil and see the future. I hope that didn't go up in smoke as it may affect one's destiny.

A month passes before I see if she will accept a peace offering. "No means no", was the gist of it. I was inclined to reply but didn't. No means no is usually fired at those that don't stop when asked – stop the sexual activity. Not stop contacting them. This is Megan though and she is probably unaware of how those three words are loaded.

A leave it another month and I have one last bash. I know that I am on ice so thin one could exhale the slightest breath and it will crack. I send a thankyou card. Now we get capitals. In text speak that I believe is shouting. She will send her dad round if I send any more "things" to her house. Laura used "things" too. Is there some secret forum where women go to find out what words to use? I ran an experiment to see what works and what doesn't on a catalogue dating app. Lots of women use the same expressions and same oddball names. Maybe I am not learning from prior mistakes. I send my mother some flowers on Mother's Day and brace myself for a call. "Stop sending me things else I will get your father on to you." Instead, I have manged to send someone some flowers that not only lasted a good while but were indeed well received.

I can't believe that Megan's dad didn't have any inkling of what was going on. I think he was staying quiet and dropping hints but then became rather more direct about it. I told her plainly that she ought to be open with her dad about the events, especially as she had given her mother every last detail. My own daughter has this habit of saying things to her mother and I find out on the grapevine weeks later. It is not great. Not much you can do about it, but it is not the best. Maybe Megan's children can return the favour. Keep your mum out of the loop on something important, just tell your father.

He may have gone a bit balmy at her and this could be the reason she was grounded. Or she was bluffing. She must explain something if she is to get him to pay me a visit. In a way I am relieved. This is not a bad outcome. No change of heart but it is all put to rest now. I wasn't going to have any further interaction anyway. I had self-moderated. However, I wouldn't mind having a calm discussion with her dad. Megan has done nothing wrong. Megan has had a romantic encounter with someone, someone of her choosing. It was not rushed. We both took time considering it. It was hardly a drunken mistake. Neither of us pressured one another. All she need do is ask her dad one question. Am I allowed to choose who I date, who I marry - do you want me to bring my prospective partners round one by and one and you say yes or no?

Megan's father shouldn't be scornful. He should be proud that he has a daughter that has most things right. She is still blighted by events at school. Bullying. Over time she will see it all differently. I had hoped to fast track the process. The flip flopping and uncertainty will give way to self-assurance eventually. She has the capacity to make a contribution to the gender debate and maybe other debates too. She needs to borrow the Chinese saying. Every long journey starts with the first step. Break it down and get on with it.

I did genuinely ask myself how I would feel if my daughter got involved with an older person. What I do know is that a skank talked the talk and led her down the garden path. Does it make it right that he was about the same age? No. He was a disingenuous skank. The truth is this. Megan's age acceptable boyfriends gave her things you would not particularly want your daughter to have whilst I gave her couscous. Whatever the others did or didn't do I showed nothing bar respect. I saw her as an equal. Nobody is ever good enough for our daughters or sons. You know why? Because we parents have invested so much time and effort in them. We spent so much time sorting things for them. We worried and willed them. We paid the price. We want. We dream. We imagine. We hope. We expect. And that is one of the many shades of love. Read the introduction in my other book. Selfishness. And the majesty magic unbelievable power of co-considerational selfishness. We gain when we give.

The beauty of living some distance from the maddening crowd is the ability to look up at the stars and see more than a handful. That is something me and Laura both liked doing, just not at the same place at the same time. Four walls, four decades later, and there is a hard to fathom TV remote to get frustrated with. This is the future and all things Laura related are tracked and monitored. Right down to the weight and composition of her ablutions. This will ensure that her underlying health conditions are kept in check, so that more time is spent in this prison-esqu paradise, than was spent in her earlier idyl. A warning to us all. Make the most of it. The first line in IP always holds true. We are the fruit from the flower from the tree. We start under ripe, become ripe, soften, wrinkle then rot and smell. We have a shelf life – a sweet one. Makeup is a wonderful thing, but you can't paper over the cracks when they are too wide and abundant.

This all made me think back to the dances in the park. Diana, sorry, Diane. I have called Diane, Diana a couple of times. Never on purpose. She was quite happy to sit back down after a dance with me. Marvellous lady. One of the things that many women fail to realise is that each follower is different, it is not easy being a leader. When you get disgruntlement, dissatisfaction and condemned, they forget that men have feelings too. It hurts. As does getting dumped by text.

I circulated, talked to everyone there each afternoon. There was also a young lady that showed interest in the dancing and hinted that she may join the fray at some point in the future. She was making notes in a diary, adding watercolours of the scene. I had a ten-minute chat with her about pottery and painting. It wasn't long before John came over - and took over. Another potential suitor for his hareem. I don't really get embarrassed, but this was toe-curling. She must have felt mobbed. I left him to it.

Some have said my partner used to put up with a lot. Sharon can only have grimaced at the constant sight of this younger appealing insta-marry-able thing called Laura that began to plonk done on their table, event after event. Laura didn't attend the winter dance nights, so a younger replacement was brought in, Emma. I know Sharon has little time for Laura. Laura got bemused by me that night and trotted off to spill the beans with Sharon. Sharon and Laura's discourse was less than a minute. Sharon ignored her off by coming back into the room and dallying away.

I arrived at a hall before the rest. John asked who I was with. "Helen, Maureen and .... Megan." "Megan ....", his voice, his face, told me all I needed to know when I announced Megan. He was not pleased/delighted. This is not some rivalry on my part. This is me wanting to push the boundaries of dance. I need that passion that Megan exhibits. John has often said, "it is the social side too". It is, but I am questioning which comes first for him, dancing or amalgamating? He has a clear run now for the whole set.

I know someone that thinks it was quite ok to pirate all kinds of films and music on the basis that they don't want to pay for it unless it is good for sure. I reckon he gets short shrift when he pays a prostitute a visit and asks to sample a 90-minute immersive experience. Then pay or most likely not another time. I mention him, for I invited Ian and his partner Dawn over for a dinner party. One load of hassle getting it all organised. Then I get a text message half-hour prior to it starting, saying they can't come. I can accept a phone call, but a text message is taking the piss. It is a real bug bear of mine. I told Megan this. Do not cancel at the last minute. Late no problem. Can't make it, but can the day after is fine. But cancelling altogether is an OCD problem of mine. My OCD is equivalent to those that know for sure that the back door, front door and all the windows are open and can see so when looking out of the car window on departure. I think we accept some forms of mental conditions especially if it has a label on it, far more than others. I plan my day around what is happening in the evening and get mentally distraught when it evaporates.

Since she had been so good after the afternoon with the live band, I began to have faith in her. I began to believe. I was no longer bracing myself for a huge let down. It is harsh to go from what we had to fuck all over night. Surely, I am not on a different planet with this? Had there been some sort of argument, disagreement, or troubling event I can understand it. The day before was golden. I got signals on a promising note - not seen before. She said 'we come as a package', namely her and Ruby. Music to my ears. I had one day where it properly felt like she was my girlfriend. The last blooming day together.

Maybe I am still not getting it. I think she felt 'iffy' about the difference in standpoint about the virus. Though it was not a dealbreaker. I can't give up my beliefs about the restrictions. In the same way, she would never give up her striving to see changes for women, feminism. We both talked in equal doses about what we cared about. We both listened to one another Keeping her parents happy was the main thing on her mind. They were not happy about her going out and living a little. I hope they are happy now and live a long, happy life in happydom.

I was tempted to say 'fuck buddy' to fuck all. It was primarily a dance and discussion buddy. The naffest films can sometimes make a significant point. Three gents sit down to watch a porn movie. One is keen to wind forward to the action. One of them objects. He wants to get to know the characters first. It makes the sex impactful. We can get a release from our urges in all kinds of ways, but that is so far removed from seriously uniting with someone.

Being open to a broad range of experimentation and exploration in dance obviously can be transferred in other quarters. Hence, there is not a single destination on the horizon. Nirvana needs change. Nirvana needs imagination. Nirvana needs creativity.

I was millimetres away from messing it up in the weeks before. I thank the cards-of-life-dealer that I had the fortitude to ply my way through the fog. If it had ended a week beforehand it would have been significantly worse from my perspective. There comes a time when it all gets too much. Too much pressure. Too much strain. Too out of balance. I need to put myself into a position where I have nothing to lose. I can't live like this anymore. I need some surety. I don't care what form it takes. Just friendship, just dance buddy, just wife, anything so long as I have something I can count on.

A once-a-week meetup for coffee would have sufficed until the lockdowns were relaxed. Anything but this. Without that, text exchanges would have petered out and feelings for one another would have faded away. It is pointless thinking about what I could have done. I have to deal with the situation and see if I can salvage anything. I threw all the chips in. Then some more. It turned out to be a fruitless endeavour.

Victims of assault are asked to hand over their phones. If they don't the police tend to drop the case. The defence will sift through every picture, every word of every message to locate something that undermines the victim's case. It is easy to find one or two things in masses of data that can be brought up to get the rapist off the hook. One or two lines of text has been used against me. All the lines surrounding it ignored. Context counts for nothing. Sometimes we spend more time arguing about what someone says than about what people have done. Stabbings, punches, murders have been side-lined by racial remarks.

What did the cheese say to the mirror? Megan records 'hello me', a joke that I replay a couple of times. Her voice on the phone is quite different to that in person. I send a reply; how do you get a bearded fellow to stop talking rubbish? Just because you have hair around your lips, it doesn't mean you can talk like a c*nt. We have a different joke bank to draw down on.

Back to the future. Laura is on the upper floor of the same institution storing Megan. Drab decor. She gets wheeled out each day into the tiny garden for a five-minute breather. There is the evening sing along to keep her spirits up, along with a hairdresser that visits every third Thursday of the month at 11. Laura's hair is the same length it has always been. Only the shine, lustre and colour are not quite there. On the plus side it matches the grey of the ceilings. That is not eating her up. She felt let down, cheated by circumstance and that promising boyfriend. She told me about what she would like to do to someone. Not me I might add. Grinding, punitive anger. I had a crazy belief that I could get to the source of the anger and be of some use.

A young dapper care worker will walk in to change Megan's adult sized nappies. She will already be up and out of bed. Not sleep walking again today but managing better than the usual four paces from the bedside on her aluminium Zimmer frame. Oh, my Mrs Megan you ought to be covered up. Megan likes to sleep naked. Pete the care worker grabs a day gown, a dowdy faded green thing and protects her modesty. Megan raises her index finger and slowly painstakingly edges it towards the centre of her chest. The finger shifts the fabric enough to re-reveal the pinkie fingernail sized blood mark. "See - this is the proof ... it really is me in that book", glancing sideways at the tipped over tomes on the lonely shelf in the room. In that book is the proof that I could dance in my youth. Megan could dance. She became good. Had she stuck around a little longer, it wouldn't have been good, it would have been great. We were just on the verge of transitioning to the next stage. I had a significant lesson all planned out for the beginning of part two. Not only did that not happen, but it was brushed aside without a mention.

You can't force stuff on her. It is like trying to catch a chicken. They dodge this way, then that way, then make a right squeal and commotion. I was teasing it out, coaxing little by little. It would require a gentle push and perseverance to get her to bloom. Any able body can learn a hundred moves. You need the right mind to give them substance. Not only does it look better to the observer, but you feel it inside.

Sadly, however many times I tried to say to her that some things are important, other things less so, it did not wash. She was having none of it. She is not entirely wrong. Practical things take precedence. How will the future pan out anyway with climate change, artificial intelligence, and population changes? I said to Megan that I would be the only person that would make it work. This is cheeky, this has some foundation of truth. I do not judge her re various activities in the past, I had dabbled decades before with certain plants that mellow you out. It was great for philosophy for it helps you think on one topic for a long time.

She doesn't take kindly to being 'picked apart'. Though who does. Her strong ability to analyse others is used to her disadvantage. She sets out to find a reason *not* to go out with someone. Then wants to find something to make the decision to end it easy. I am never going to see her again, so it doesn't matter what I say. I might as well add that it could be copying the same control that her mother has. To be the one that wears the trousers and be the one to dump. Cold and brutally.

The one good thing I can say is that I probably have more imperfections than she. Our strengths/weaknesses complement each other. Thus, our pairing was good.

I think we started some fifty conversations but completed none. She simply scatters off in a new direction. Being open is wonderful, but I am accustomed to discretion. Some things are best kept secret. Certain details are sacrosanct – not to be shared with others.

I would like a relationship of equals. It is more of a principle, an aim. I haven't mapped out what it entails precisely yet. Regardless of that I have always seen the merit of putting yourself first, then your partner followed by your children. Precedence seems odd at first but if the husband and the wife are happy, then the children will be too. Get that wrong and all become disillusioned.

So many people plot and plan a future. An ideal future. Sadly, society is littered with single parents, the bereaved, blended families, the swindled, the stuck alone - all kinds. Relationships do thrive, but usually transform into something different to what was hoped for. We see those that manage it and use those as examples, it gives us belief. False belief. It is possible, but unseen compromises are overlooked. She said her dad was happy playing drums and playing with train sets. Is he happy though? It is assumed so. Assumed.

Laura tells me about her little niece and whilst doing so her face lit up like a Christmas tree. I covered all bases when I set my stall out with her in the section in the other book. I said that I would step up to the plate and do what is needed so her career could continue unimpeded. I had to make sure there was nothing that ruled me out. You will see that despite all these upsides I was under no illusions that the chance of us two getting together was absurdly unlikely. It was a one in a million shot. To be fair impractical in some regards.

I can't imagine what it would be like to be involved in an accident where someone gets killed or injured. You would replay events over and over and see mistakes you made. These sorts of regrets live with us. However, there are things we didn't do, that we could have made more effort with that bug us dearly right up to our final days. They eat away at us and keep us feeling bitter. We regret getting our priorities wrong.

I had made the curiosity illustration, reward gadget, and boredom instrument many years ago. Only the selfishness one remained. I could have made it years prior or years after, but no, I happened to make it that summer. I only mentioned it in passing and had no idea of the consequences. I wasn't even sure how to illustrate it until a few weeks before. That would suffice in getting Laura to zip off home and take a gander at my text. There is zero shame in wanting. There is no shame in things not happening. Life rarely pans out the way we thought it would. Life's a bitch, then you marry one.

Tentatively I engaged with Laura again. She was outright stressed and apprehensive about handling a parents evening. I said to her that I loved parents' evenings. She asked as a child or parent. As a parent. Her acknowledgment only added more confirmation regarding my belief. I have an inkling of what caused the separation. I am often not wrong. I know the cure. Laura is a bullshitter. She had me a few times. She is good. I mean, real good, but I remember details. I am also a poker player. I reckon her ex just had enough of it. She convinced him one time too many and then he left. Maybe he had an affair. I don't know. Anything but this being frustratingly misled over and over. She is also adept at seeing off sniffers, pests, double glazing salesmen etc. That is great but I think she might be too adept, too accustomed to shooing people away.

She will never know what I would have told her. No clue about the relevance and utility of certain perspectives. I would have held out my hand and let her see my ring at eye level. "Now Laura when you put your heels on you get a different perspective. You can now see the dust on your shelf." That small change is a different perspective. You can see the ring differently too as I lower it down a little. I can give you another way of seeing things. However, you choose. In the same way you can put your heels on or take them off, you retain control, retain autonomy. Un-controlling assistance that is not advising people what to do. I am talking bullshit myself here, she needs none of my help, it is simply help in a similar vein to what I have given others successfully in the past.

Helen kindly fits in a visit. She asked me if I was in a relationship with Megan. I said nothing and gave little away. Helen pointed out that others involved with Megan just disappeared, vanished without trace. "Perhaps she knows what she is looking for." Helen was going to be more cautious – no more coming over for dances. I might be shunned now, and everyone will close ranks. We will see. Paranoia can set in. We can believe narcissistically that people are talking about us. Most are not and if they are it is only very briefly. This is to set the record straight in my head, not anyone else's. I know that. We imagine all sorts, but in truth people care predominately about themselves, not what others are up to or not. Many do not even notice someone's absence let alone care about the reasons. I said that I was ashamed of myself. In truth there was shame on my part, but not for sending messages. I didn't value Megan enough in the early days. I wanted to swap her for Laura prior to lockdown and didn't fully appreciate what I had until half-way through our few months of dancing together. I had someone that was more bountiful than Laura, by far, but didn't realise it at first. I was too focused on the Laura experiment. The person that I have been least respectful to is Helen. I had to stab her in the back a couple of times for the cause.

Sending that final thankyou card was the straw that broke the camel's back. There was one mystery that remained. I couldn't let it go. I had a hunch but couldn't say for sure. The thankyou card confirmed it. In wanting this confirmation, I paid a heavy price. Never mind, we are all soon forgotten and there will be other storms in teacups to get us in a stew about.

I told her a few times that I would always fight for her. I made my case. I tried to make us a thing. I tried to restore the friendship. Lots apparently sent people unrequested gifts during the lockdown. That along with domestic violence, divorces and self-harm went up dramatically. Not being able to go nightclubbing, to pubs and bars limits their usual human interaction. Is it a justification? Maybe not, but it is a reason. People with partners didn't give two hoots about the singletons, they never understood how isolated others felt.

Having all these claims thrown at me, knocked me for six. It made me uncertain of myself. Am I a nasty horrid piece of work that has overstepped the mark in a big way? I know I have never done anything terrible.

However, a thief is a thief whether they steal a pack of sweets of a hundred gold bars. One thing can tip the balance and make people qualify as a harasser. Maybe I will try a different approach the next time. If there is the slightest murmuration, I will ghost out, blank them immediately. No thanking people anymore, no trying to apologise, and I won't send flowers again; they were a lot of money for zilch.

I scroll the news channels and come across a piece in the Stylist about harassment. Better check this out and see how bad a person I am. The attacker entered Laura's apartment building with a spare key fob over 100 times in a month, sometimes spending the night in the building's corridors. The attacks resulted in a trip to hospital due to broken ribs, damage to her jaw and extensive bruising and swelling. On it goes. The names of the victims were changed - the final coincidence in this story.

STYLIST
Laura's story

Laura*, 26, from Belfast was violently assaulted by her ex-boyfriend after

Megan's story

Megan*, 28, from Edinburgh, didn't realise she was being stalked at first. "I was

When John departs the famous five will gather to dig a large hole befitting the status of this great man. Megan will be at the bottom of the pit with mud on her forehead from wiping her brow. As Megan fills each bucket of spoils, they will be lifted at speed by the rope attached to Emma's bicycle. She will be peddling furiously to power the lighting too. Laura will be delegating and making sure Beth is keeping the refreshments coming. Sometime after Sharon broke ground they stop when 30ft below the surface. This is not because John is a large person, nor because he had a substantial beer belly, but because deep down he is a lovely person.

The Eulogy. "He said every meal is a banquet, blardy, blardy, blah." "He had his fans, one on the ceiling and two in his computer." "For Sharon the loss will be noticeable, having him around was like a bus man's holiday; pulling teeth."

"I'm still standing", says Elton John. I now have to summon the will to find another dance partner. I will show them what dancing is all about too. Well, what I think it is all about, many are quite happy with what they do. I will find someone that has the same qualities as Megan. Hopefully she will have the same vigour. Someone that also wants to enjoy dance more than revel in the politics. I may even have a go at teaching. Unlikely, but why not. If I do, I will show those that come that there are no rules. You do not have to be regimented. We can deviate a little, not just stick to moves that are to the book. You can fuse, you can mix and match. I will teach people to lead and follow. I will instil the belief that we can find our own style. We can have fun. I know how. I know the ingredients that is needed to eliminate the boredom that can creep in. I do know what it was like to be a beginner thus I can show leaders how to get out of the catch-22. Namely not knowing enough moves to lead a full song. There are shortcuts. I will get the best out of people. Believe me. I am not suggesting that Matt and Sarah ought to change things, if they do it may alienate the core group of people that attend. You can't please everyone and the harder you try the worse it gets.

Nearing the end of the last of the three dance-in-the-park meets, I approached Hazzle and suggested we do a whip round for Matt and Sarah. We gathered in quite a bit; people were more generous than I expected. I had overheard Hazzle gushing about Matt, "He is suuuch a good teacher". He is. He is also the laziest teacher in the region. Not once have I ever seen him dance with anyone bar Sarah. Debbie would work her arse off, making sure she had a dance with every attendee – as many as she could each week. This enabled her to get a handle on how well the teaching is going. Only by dancing with people, can you see first-hand what the issues are. There are some striking issues in Matt's franchise. Followers don't follow. They are guided by clockwork and guesswork. I turn the lady 360 and now have my hand up high with theirs. I want to go under my own arm and do a turn. The lady makes a guess and starts to turn! Oh my god. Do what you want then. I want them to hold still. The difference between this and what I can do with Megan/Laura is like the difference between a computer and an abacus.

Some say following is not easy. Let me tell you, it is easy unless you have been leading all your life. Learning to follow with style is a different matter entirely. Put it this way. I have got a lady to follow quite well in a couple of hours. I have never seen anyone pick leading up in a couple of hours. You can argue as much as you like but please remember I am talking about learning to follow with someone that can lead proficiently. When lead sharing takes off, both men and women can get an appreciation of how difficult the roles are. There might be less criticism. I have been a little critical myself of some here. A little unfair as most have been cordial and instructive. Most have been good to get to know. That is both leaders and followers.

We grumble about other dancers rather than say hang on, maybe I could adapt or get something from this style. Artist Michelle was gradually tuning into my flow. She was making an effort. Think of it this way. When you lead you can have a bigger say in how the dance shall go. If you want to of course. This is why lead sharing is a revolution. It may seem like a gimmick at first that anyone could have come up with, but it has profound consequences.

When I mess about it is often for a reason. For fun and to make a point I would sometimes stop half-way through a move. I have their hand up at my left shoulder. Usually, it will stay there for no more than a quarter of a second before I push down and out to my right side. They know the move; they know what is coming. So, they turn out immediately on their own volition before I give the lead. But I haven't pushed out, I let go instead. She is then caught out. Shocked, surprised and disconnected from me. Megan/Laura and all those that have had this bit of entertainment put on them before will wait. In other words, I am leading, they are following.

As for making mistakes, it is always the leader's fault. Always. Either they gave a poor lead, or it was simply their fault. Leaders; take it on the chin. Recover it. Do the move again a bit slower. Forget about it. Carry on. Whatever. There is a skill curve. Followers start off good as they haven't got much of a clue. Then they get progressively worse. To fix them they have to start right back at the beginning, learning to follow. Go where you are led. If I pull you in, my left hand - your right hand, you step forward turn a little and put your right hand on the leader's shoulder. If I pull you in right hand to right hand, you don't turn at all, just step forward in line. If he moves his right foot forward, you move your left foot back. If I hold a hand out, you move to grab it. And that is it. There is obviously a little more to it than that, but that is the essence of it. A follower may have to learn a range of signals relating to specific flavours of Jive for more advanced moves.

If you want it to look good, then put effort into style, not psychic predictions of what you think they might want you to do. The only mistake a follower can do is move when they didn't feel a lead.

This man woman thing will change of course. I would teach both, right from the start to lead and follow. It will be tiring, it will be demanding, but it will be the way.

A new way. A better way. No more sexism in dancing. Women are allowed to drive you know. Many are permitted to get a job. Some are allowed to leave their home without a male guardian accompanying them. Megan has shown that it can be done. If Megan can do it, anyone can do it.

If you asked me out of all those that I know, who is the best dancer, it would be difficult question to answer. I could tell you who has the most passion, or who is the most graceful. I could tell you who has the most technical ability or the most potential. I could tell you who is the most fun or the most sought after. But the best? There is no best. If I had a new idea to try, I would grab hold of Megan. Get it right, then express it with Laura. It is a marginal difference though. If I were to spend a year on a desert island and could take someone with me, there would be no question that Megan would be my first pick. She is grand in so many areas.

How does one dance like a twenty-year old? Is there a clear distinction between a young dancer and an old one? Of course there is. Is it psychological? They may have beauty of youth and appear to be nicer to dance with. However, in general they are far easier to move, to turn, to control. Lighter and less resistance. Time slows down as we age so perhaps their clock runs quicker and therefore they can respond quicker. To emulate a youthful one, one would need to flow with the gentlest touch. Hone your balance, hone your turns, and stop over thinking it.

Lead sharing doubles things up. You can double it again. You can lead them leading you. This is distinct from the lady leading when they shouldn't be. It is recrafting a move so that you are moving them in the way they would do if they were leading you. Confused?

You probably would be. Let me explain. I invite the lady to move behind me with our left hands in contact. We cavort with our right arms out to the side. I lead her into this position. After a few moments I push backwards, and we both spin out. To lead them leading you I have to circumvent the need to signal. Partner dancing has signals. Signals to give your partner an idea of where to move, what hand to grab and when to turn. You can't make a follower provide a signal when you are leading them leading you, so one needs to rejig moves. It is not a problem. It just needs some consideration. Thus, I pull the lady in front of me, both now facing forward. I step to the left and take her left hand. I step right and tuck her hand behind her. Now she is in the same spot as I would be if I were leading her. We cavort with our right arms briefly then I push out. So, I led her leading me.

I told you I play golf one handed - with just one club and one ball. I would walk up to the tee and whack the ball a fair distance. If I don't scuff, it, slice it or hook it, it makes quite an impression on those that struggle using two hands. Golf one handed, pool one handed, I can even play darts one handed. There is a one-armed gent that spends most of his time watching us dance. I reckon a study of mirror moves would enable him to level up enough to qualify as an equal. You can have a code of conduct that states you are inclusive but in practice you are far from it. At my dance gig I would show a one-armed person what they can do to compensate. As an example, you can bring the lady's arm up and rest it on your shoulder, leave it there then take the other hand. Takes too many words to prescribe it but with a bit of thought, mirroring, leading them leading you and so forth there is plenty for a three-minute song.

I did play a trick on Megan. Megan being Megan fell for it hook line and sinker. I stole the concept from a football player that advertised crisps. I held Megan's hands in front of me and pushed her backwards. I pushed and pushed as she tried to resist and push back. She built up a head of steam and began to overpower me. Pushing me now, rearwards. Gary would run at 90% speed to allow a defender to think they can catch him. When it mattered, he would go at 100% and get past to score a crucial goal. Megan now thinks she is stronger than me. She suggested that she could beat me at an arm wrestle. A few weeks pass and we had an arm wrestle of sorts that she duly lost. This was a game within a game that had a purpose.

I never set out to run an experiment. It had already started. It took me three attempts to work out how to talk to Laura. I knew there must be a way. I described elsewhere how it is like being down a coal mine with no headlamp and a toothpick trying to find a soft vein of rock. Most dancers will say hello, smile and look at you. Not Laura. She would have her head a quarter down and a quarter to the left, then look up briefly when doing the move in hand. I challenged her to a staring competition. This went well. A good twenty seconds or more, I don't know, but she looked at me more thereafter. I then wanted to get her to smile at me. "Smile, ... Smile Laura." Nope. I commenced the practice move and stopped with her in hold. "I am not going to move until you smile." She gave me this comical sarcastic gurning grin and we then completed the move. I nearly fell off the chair backwards even though I was standing up when she did smile at me. It was not long after things had died down following the ruckus.

I got her name wrong for a while. "Hello Lauren", "Bye Lauren", for weeks. I sit down next to Laura and Jill arrives. "This is my mate, Lauren." Lifting her head skywards, "Actually, my name is Laura", she corrects me. It is as if it doesn't matter that I have it wrong, but on no account must others have it wrong also. The thing is, I do like her at this stage. She is alright. When you get a conversation going it is good. I link arms. At the concerts I would do the arm link turn jig a few times then swap around, other arm and turn a few times the other way. Irish jig maybe is what it is called. Not sure. I could do this with five or six people in turn. I even had one fellow run down from the stands to join in. With Laura it was different. She upped the pace to a rather hazardous degree. We span around together like this, fast, more than once. This wowed me. She is fun. She always looks happy when she is dancing. It is not put on.

I am sitting next to her, again, like most weeks for the few minutes before the start of class. I laugh at what seems like two people trying to escape the wrath of a giant plastic bag. Invalid 'dancing'. Laura asks me what I am chuckling at. Then some warm dialog. Lots of little things, though nothing to write home about. Then she takes her turn in front of me and mentions a weekend dancing trip. ".. but I am single." I know she is single. But her saying so right there, right then, triggers something. I am thinking I will go with you. It was then that I began to think about Laura. Possibilities. Potential. Dance weekends. Sailing. Let's play some games. Let's see what tricks work and which do not. I am pretty sure she will be immune to most of them. Nevertheless, she can't be immune to them all. I have progress markers. She has never used my name, not once, not spoken it ever. If that changes it would be one.

Week after week, I tap her hand very gently and ply softly - just briefly. I watch. Nothing. No reaction. Odd. This is forbidden by the way. Valentine's day is an opportunity. I get a card.

"Tell Laura I ..

bit cheesy, but happy Valentine's Day"

I am somewhat nervous about giving it to her. She asks, "What's this then?" I dash off for a dance with Helen. The second half of the class starts, and I am now even more nervous and concerned. However, I did a little test in the first half. A standard curiosity test. I tell her that I had a bit of a revelation at the last band night. This was true. She asks me what. I feign to give her an explanation. She moves on down the line. When she completes the circuit back to me again, she asks about this revelation. I tell her that I am going to just do my thing, the slower smoother dance style regardless of how many detractors I get. Some like it a lot, an odd few stare in slight wonderment after. She came at me wanting to know. This is a positive indicative thing. She did not forget and brush me aside.

One by one the dancers are peeling off and Laura is heading my way. I am now in for something. Has the card made any noise? I hoped she is not irritated by it. Something remarkable happens. First, I said I like the move we were learning that night, she said she thought it would be one for me. Then she had my hand and did the same rub tap as I was doing to her over the preceding weeks. Only more warmly. Small things - big impression. Let's clarify. I am still a million miles from anything happening 'romantically' or otherwise. This is just friendly stuff. It is an experiment nothing more. The only problem is that one can become quite immersed in it. An infatuation arises, a fantasy that is nice and troublesome to contend with.

In years gone by, I ran a self-experiment. I followed my attention relentlessly. Life became very strange. I would notice every switch of attention. This was most revealing. We are an animal machine. It took a while to get in the habit of doing it and unfortunately several years to return to normal. This is nothing akin to mindfulness or meditation. It is intercepting the thought processes themselves. Noticing every interrupt. Every sound, everything that grabs your attention. When you blink you do not notice the world going black every few seconds. When you pay attention to it you will. Translate that to all other aspects of your self and you may get an idea of how life is very different when you do this. It is not better. It is quite awful.

The Laura experiment included a look at inner emotions. My emotions and the effect of desire. The effect of infatuation and wanting. The effect of heartache. Many things came from it. I may be rather stupid but the falling for someone well outside of my normal 'type' was profound. I am sure many others already understand what was only beginning to dawn on me. It took a long time for the appeal of Megan to surface. When it did it was savage. People grow on you. Megan challenged central beliefs of what constituted attractiveness to me. I did like Megan from day one. I liked her a lot. When I asked her, her age, I immediately thought, "that is no good then".

Laura's dress sense is impeccable. Feminine, professional and it shows a lot of effort without being ultra-vain. Megan goes to great lengths to look ridiculous. Not only that but walks funny and has the most odd-shaped legs. I could elaborate. I am hardly an alpha male, mega handsome critter, yet I found myself laughing at her, but that turned into desire. If I had a magic wand, could look her up and down and change one thing, yes, I would alter something. Me, my stupidity. As for her, I would not change a single thing. Not one thing about her. Some things I most certainly would not have in any other proportion for they are beyond perfect. The more I think about it the more crazy it seems to be critical. She is just the right height, no defacements, but ultimately her vitality is what will shine the longest.

There are bad writing awards given to works of fiction that show the most bonkers descriptions of people bonking. Awards for the most cringeworthy accounts of people having sex. Long pole is substituted for penis etc. You can look them up yourself, so I feel no urge to pen more about it. The film 'Blue is the warmest colour' has a lengthy intense sex scene. Most people find most sex scenes dull and dreary. In this case the only relevance the graphic nature of those sex scenes have is borne out in the later part of the film. It made the break-up feel much more significant. We understood it fully. The termination of their relationship had meaning because we saw how intertwined they were previously. No words, not even a graphic account, can really give a reader much sense of my consternation. My loss. Perhaps our loss.

The real bugbear is that I never got to uncover the essence of it. I would have needed another few weeks to explore it, analyse it and understand it fully. I know what has turned me on in the past, I have explored all of that thoroughly. That hasn't exactly changed, but this is an entirely new avenue that has opened up. A frighteningly stirring avenue. As for Laura, it is the concept of Laura rather than Laura herself that matters. It is what she represents. It is an illusion. She had far more initial appeal than Megan. It all changed for I uncovered appeal that was not plain for me to see before. I suppose there is the meal deal. What is better, an excellent main or an excellent pudding? Or the holiday conundrum, a trip to the Caribbean or a trip to Mount Fuji? Both thrilling. Whatever the case some things on the table suit our unique tastebuds far more than others. A heck of a lot more.

I have been longing for an alliance with an 'interactive creature' for some time. I see that as having more value than anything else in the world. No material item can compensate. Malcolm said he has little interest in women now. I thought to myself, no sportscar, no private jet, no football match, no nothing has the ability to pique as much interest. For the most part, whilst sex can be at the centre it is not the biggest element. I just like talking, dancing, being with those that sparkle. Megan proved to be the one that turned the longing for such an alliance into reality. At times it felt unreal. Surreal. Over the years I can count on one hand the number of people that I formed a deep association with like this. Melanie and Juliet in English class. A singer in Kenya and a few others. It is quite distinct from other great friendships that have been in abundance. What me and Megan had was rare and I have been about long enough to know that.

Each person that comes down the line points out that my shoelaces are undone. So, once in a while, I will put my foot forward and request that they do them up for me. On average it is the fifth lady that will oblige. Tonight, Helen gets down and has the satisfaction of doing her good deed of the day. She stands not that high off the floor so needs not bend down too far. Lots of people had a little laugh at this including Laura. One dude was mortified/impressed/shocked going by the look he gave me.

This brings me on to gentlemanly behaviour. I made a big mistake with Laura. I showed her far too much reverence. Instead of reverence, it would have paid to have 'taken the piss out of her' far more. A lot more. I gave her too many compliments. If someone thinks they are above you, too attractive for you, or you feel out of your depth then de-elevating is essential. Bring them down to your level. Get them doing things for you. Get them to open and hold the door for you. Rather than buy them a drink, ask them to buy you one. Get them to hold things for you. Get them to sort things out. I used to walk into a pub, take my coat off and without thinking hand it to my partner to hang up. We stayed together for more years than Megan has existed. That lockdown was a real pest. I had so many things lined up to try with Laura. I had reached a point where she showed a little fondness towards me, and I could have built on that.

Lots of people have spoken about small things. Strangers that make a little effort. People that give a few minutes of their time. People that thank you. People that show a modicum of respect. People that compliment you. People that help you up when you stumble over. People that take on board what you are saying. Karen slipped over on some ice. Three teenagers rushed over and helped her back on to her feet. Her whole view of teenagers changed in that instance. She must have told fifty people how grateful she was.

I have known all this for a long time. Writing about it in relation to Laura crystallised in me the impact it has on us. Some will point out how they appreciate their partner putting out the rubbish, running the vacuum over, doing little things without prompting. It is not doing such things all the time but noticing that it would be a help when it is obvious that they are tired and in need of help. I say this not to be pious but because it was Laura that brought it to my attention and gave me the impetus to examine the power of little things. Little things can change the entire impression we have of a person, a race, a creed, or a whole community. Your small seemingly insignificant action can have a profoundly positive impact. Laura got me thinking about other things too. Things of significance. To me anyway. She gave me dancing back too.

My partner would eye-roll me frequently. Not caring about what your partner is interested in, speaks volumes. I got to the point where I would only talk about my passions to other people. That was the only way she got to hear about them, when listening on the side-lines. That was a big thing I found refreshing with Megan, we would have two-way conversations. Sting recorded an album on the volcanic island of Montserrat. This brought a German named Marc there. He being a huge fan wanted to visit and soak up the vibes, to be where Sting had hung out. The trip was paid for by his girlfriend. That is telling. She had saved up and made it happen. She had no great affection for the singer but understood Marc's obsession. I had a dance or two with an eighty-year-old local, jolly fun dance to live steel drum band music. It took me a lot of persuasion to get the girlfriend up to dance in front of so many spectators. She turned out to be quite competent groover, most surprised was I.

I was getting a bit tired of the weekly dancing. I had been doing it for a long time. So many classes going over the same things or roughly the same things. I was having to say to myself that I need the exercise. I would drag myself there and clock watch. Glad when it is all done and glad to go home. This is jolly unfair and disrespectful to the wonderful people that attend. However, it was how I felt. It just was not going anywhere. Laura metamorphosised things like a caterpillar into a butterfly. It transpired that Megan had the inner beauty that captured my enthusiasm to really strive, to expand it greatly. I became keen as mustard now for every dance thing now that I had Megan about.

"Ken won't be my bitch", complains Jo. Brave enough to join the army but not gallant enough to make Jo content. I told Megan my plan to entice the men to have a go at following and thus share the lead. Her response? She kissed me. It obviously draws on the desire to impress. Also, the desire to dance with the ice-creams. Megan is in the bag. Laura will soon follow, and Beth could soon be up to speed with her devout desire to dance. Jo and Megan are not the only ones hot to trot, quite a few women are accomplished leaders.

I honestly found it fun and, in some ways, quite relaxing once I had the basics mastered. I whole new experience. Let someone else be in command for a change and have the most thinking to do. Megan soon became more assertive. She also had to learn to get ready to catch me. The leader needs to move themselves in to position ready for where the follower will end up after spinning out. She worked out how hard to yank me forward then around so I rotated cleanly and parked in front of her.

I would give Megan the odd hint, remind her of a potential move to do next, not worrying about the pause. She would stop and get a bit flummoxed. "No problem Megan, how about ..." To see her advance was great. More than anything, her willingness to try was the most golden aspect.

Some men might worry about their image. At first. Novelty wears off and gets replaced by admiration. For a start you will find the beginners moves interesting again, the same as when you first learnt to lead. You will at least get a few months of classes that are not dull and dreary going over the endless cycle of simple moves that you know inside out leading. Ultimately you will dance more.

I do remember three girls turn up who were stubborn as heck. They were most unimpressed by the whole thing. I am pretty sure they took umbrage at having to follow with the men in charge. Now this was a good few years back. Things have moved on since women chained themselves to railings and brought down the king's horse at Epsom. One lady exclaimed a hoorah when Matt let the women have a bit of a 'lead' within a move. I know there is some muted wish for change. My thinking is this. If a new lady arrives and asks why the men are leading, and women are following, we can say, "there are some that share the lead".

Greece, sometime last century I slotted my fingers into the fingers of a Belgian girl. Interlocked like this is great, dancing becomes fractionally more intimate. Me and Megan would perpetually slide into this silky weave without any conscious thought. I gave the Belgian girl an extended snog before making my way out. I saw her in my periphery the next day. I didn't want to be rude to the person I was talking to so didn't properly acknowledge her. She thought I was blanking her. In the few seconds that it took to make my excuses, she was gone. I went outside and there was no sign of her. How annoying. The last day of the holiday rolls around and I see her walk into the bar, she ignores me. I ask her friend, "what is the matter with her?", "Isn't it obvious". The Belgian then gets a can't-believe-my-luck-twool to dance with her and uses our finger embrace. He is properly grinning and jizzed up. She is only dancing with him to show me. I have a flight to catch, but I go over to her. Explain, apologise then gave her some well-deserved flattery. She giggles. She is happy. I made peace.

I have always made every effort to make peace with people. I have rarely failed to do so. I am confident that I managed to, largely, with Laura. I never will with Megan. I recall having a bit of a run in with a car boot trader. I saw him a month later and we had a chat. His wife said, "I thought you weren't going to talk to him anymore". He simply shrugged his shoulders and we both new. What is the point. All good again. I suppose Matt was right. I do have a pattern of behaviour. This is it. I make amends, I sort things, I rectify the problem the best I can. And I do it over and over whenever it is necessary. Maybe I am not as perfect as he and make more waves. Friends come and go, enemies accumulate.

The first time I introduced this finger slotting business, it didn't go quite as smoothly as I wanted it to. I was behind Megan and in the zone. I had to break from the trance to organise the detail of it. This was a little frustrating as this was the second time that I 'felt it'. I jumped out of the mind state unfortunately and could not get back into it. Maybe there is a similarity to hypnosis? I just don't know, but this 'feeling it' had another overtone. Desire. There was no desire the previous time with the other lady.

Edith Piaf's Regret Rein invites us to do a slow back roll. Left hand to right hand. Bring hands forward and turn to each other's backs. Make slow sure contact, rolling through. I stopped when we had our backs pressed against each other, then performed a form of aerial move. It is one of two that is just about passable as safe. Aerial moves are usually dis-allowed in most dance halls. I linked arms behind me and bent forward lifting her off the ground. I found a Reggae version of the song, a live recording that is divine. Megan being Megan had me on her back too, many times doing this slightly silly stunt. I did trust her. She is quite durable. The flop is another fun one. You can do it by surprise with someone that you get on with. Simply waltz in front, take both hands behind you, lower yourself down then flop them on to your back and stumble about whilst doing a few turns. Megan would also give me a piggy-back and we would charge around the room. And around the gardens until she was exhausted.

I made a huge mistake, I am forlorn. It was all my fault. All of it. I didn't take heed of what she had said the week before. I got carried away. At least nobody got hurt. No one was injured. Nobody died. Lots of others are suffering a harsher bereavement than me. It so feels like a death. A few words that were never understood.

I have seen lots who shut people out abruptly, over one piddly verbal infraction. I lived in hope. I tried to work things out. All in vain. It usually works. Megan will be pleased that I am banned. Not jubilant but feel that it is justified. Oh well. Worse things happen at sea.

There was many a house that rested upon the cliff. As time went by, the sea reclaims the land. First the garden goes, followed by the conservatory then the house itself. The newly formed beach has a towering box regularly placed on it for a Punch and Judy show. Two pieces of wood form a cross upon which invisible strings are attached. A puppeteer personifies the control of the dainty doll.

The saddest thing I witnessed was the hasty shift from true-to-herself Megan to truly conformist. A decline into a clone of the normal, dull, stereotypical, average, ordinary, boring, everyday girl on the street. Same, same, dull, no conviction. Out went the hairy arm pits etc, out went the thinking for herself. She started to just do as she was told, do what is expected, do the same as all the others. She began to follow orders and do what others wanted her to do. For their benefit. It is a shame for she was never tentative about challenging me in any debate. Maybe the fact that she was a challenging sort was part of the appeal.

She was way beyond simply having someone to dance with. We both crave someone that can stimulate us. There for us without being suffocating. Humdrum won't cut it for long. Good enough is fine for a while, but it withers when those vital things are missing. It is that key in the lock thing. It is not that someone must be extraordinary, but extraordinary to us personally. Love.

Those leans we did personify the support we give to our partner. Not possible alone. It takes balance, trust, and co-operation. We took it in turns to be the one shifting their weight to keep it stable. We can give one another a lot, learn from each other. I envisaged Megan catching up in most areas and overtaking me. Not just in dancing. She is a valuable individual like a rare, misprinted postage stamp.

Aladdin had his lamp to rub and make a wish, all I seem to rub, is people up the wrong way. I was prepared to go the extra mile or three to keep the friendship alive, hence all the futile attempts to see if there was any mending possible. I still have plenty of friends. You know the score, some drift away, or we move away. I have to say this one was particularly cherished, by a wide margin. The first in a long while that showed reciprocal respect. I suppose it was when she sat on the side of me and gave me a prolonged radiant gaze that was flattering. That aroused a solid persistent newfound hope. Affection, wanting, acceptance, comfort, uplifting and reassuring. This can fade when the fundamentals are not there. It had for me and now it feels like a rebirth. I feel like I am someone that counts again. Many people have helped me in so many ways over the years. I tried to say to Megan that she threw away a get out of jail free card. She may have never needed it, but it gives us confidence sometimes to go ahead with something knowing that if all else fails you have someone to fall back on.

This writing will add to my bad man image. I might as well run with it. Be bad and acknowledge it. John steered Matt to get me gone. Laura was a good sport and can keep her head held high. I owe her for the inspiration. Out of all this, people will take up lead sharing and see that it adds so much to the thrill of dancing. It is a simple idea that needed to be tried and evaluated. It is the business. Without Laura I would not have come up with it. As for Megan, she can brush this all aside. She will have quickly partnered up with someone remarkable.

I debated for a while whether it is fair to include some things. I have met many single women in their 30's and there is one common theme that runs deep. They can be perplexed. Asking is it men, circumstances, luck, are they expecting too much? There is one thing they have in their control. Themselves. We all can ask ourselves what do I offer before seeking out what others offer us.

Megan was unwilling to get too emotionally entrenched with me. I told her about pain. It is just pain. Pain reminds you of being alive. Revel in it. Sense it. If you want a boring, null, benign existence, then so be it. Play it safe, stay safe. No risk, no reward, no uncertainty, no investment, no treasure. Never follow your heart, stick to sensible, stick to what others think is best.

We are entering a new age of caution, cancel and over reaction. Those that ostracise friends when they don't agree with them find their friend count dropping to zero. Where is the understanding, the acceptance, the leeway, and clemency? You have mad ideas, mad opinions too. Why can't others as well? You probably agree really, just haven't found common ground. Instead of thrashing it out we over react and cut them out of our lives. We over react to mistakes, we over reacted to this virus, we over react to comments in the media, we over react to items in the news. How did we get here? It is not without reason. We invented mobile phones to talk to one another and now find kids in school pressing one another for nude pictures. We have some getting the wrong idea entirely about sex. The problems are real, however we over react. There is an abundance of caution. Guilty until proven innocent and even then, we see it as no smoke without fire and stay cautious. This will all turn ugly. So, pack up your troubles and go dancing whilst you still can.

I find myself in a position with nothing to lose. I can say what I like. They can't ban me again. I am free. I have always been free. I respect others and do my utmost to avoid harming others. However, freedom is about have the gall and confidence to take a calculated risk.

One thing is for sure, one thing is absolutely clear, no matter what anyone says, nothing bad happened. Nothing bad whatsoever. It was lucky that our paths crossed. I had an affinity towards her that was not based on the usual thing that draws me towards women, superficial presentation.

If I had done anything as bad as what Arry had done, he committed a sexual assault albeit a minor one, then yes fair dinkum. When I reach 110, I can look back over my life and think that the worst I did was send roses to an English rose and an orchid to an agrestal uncut diamond. Plus, a thankyou card for the understanding. Oh, and of course a platinum beast too for the idea. If she had an ounce of sense, she would have put her hand out and requested a few more. Someone will teach her.

I am not going to count the couple of colourful messages. One was quite sarcastic, the other somewhat insensitive. Big deal. She was a self-professed snowflake. A light bulb filament is more apt. Gets hot and poof - gone in a puff of smoke. It was my fault, I had to turn the voltage up a bit to get her to glow, she is bright, I need her to shine, but I overdid it, and it went pop.

I sent flowers as they are used in my happiness illustration. Flowers have roots. The stem represents the thing that supports us - relationships. We attempt to fill the head with petals. The more petals in place the more content we become. A petal may be a career, a house, a hobby, a fascination explored. At the centre - the head, our health.

Megan and I had those conversations that many will, getting to know one another. Our family, our upbringing, trips to relaxed basic living in Romania and temporary homelessness in France. Rescuing animals and the ways of the world. Plenty of things to talk about especially as we grew up in different decades. It was nice to have a debating companion. She could hold her own. I have spoken with hundreds of women at length, and it is so often either one-sided, self-orientated or plain dull. Fine and absorbing for one night, but often that is that, only fine for one night. I was preparing the ground to adapt her mindset to handle critical thinking. She had the capacity. I liked her suggestion relating to a certain hub she often watches on the internet. This talk would bore the pants of many, it would frustrate and irritate a few, but enthral and satisfy those that care about getting to the core of many issues. It takes all sorts and we each have our passions, some football, weightlifting and body building protein pills. That is super, but if that is it, then many feel hungry for more. More provoking, more substantial, more interactive. I said I wanted an interactive creature, and I had one here in mind and body and with terrific interplay between the two. It is annoying. It is very annoying that she is now a lost cause. It took a while to accept it. All my effort getting her to that stage in dance was a waste. I can't grumble too much about the lost investment as she helped me substantially in the sex thing.

I am sure most of us have tried to describe love. We can love our football team. We can love our pets. We can have unconditional love for our children. I think the love towards Laura was an infatuation love that hovers there for a while. If it is the same love for Megan it seems to have hovered for a lot longer and has stayed in place. There was a noticeable switch from one type to another. She said she was drawn towards me. I was gradually drawn more and more towards her. You have no idea how much.

Infatuation is no big deal, millions up and down the land get hooked by it. It passes. We move on. If I look back, out of all the encounters, only a tiny percentage were major losses. A temporary burning desire that left little trace after. It didn't help that I lost a companion, a dance buddy, and a 'lover' all in one bundle, all in one go.

Some say we should live in the moment. But I like being nostalgic from time to time. I also like looking forward to things in the future as well. Can we have balance, an equitable portion of all three? All are good.

I plant trees in the garden and look forward to the day they produce peaches and cherries. As I scan my field, I remember planting some years back and deciding where to put them. I also like seeing the progress made already rather than keep saying "this will look good next year or the year after".

We need not forget the past and try to wipe it from our minds. I have danced freely in the past. I immerse myself in it now and will work on things that will come to fruition in the future. I take what Megan provided forward. She made me happy. Whilst writing this has been a form of self-therapy, that doesn't mean I am going to just forget her. No chance, I will always retain a fond memory of the encounter. I am so glad I met her.

As I say, she is bright. I told her so. She may have failed one or two, nearly all, of her exams at school but they are a piss poor measure of one's ability. It is not guidance she needs but someone to test her. I had belief, assurance, and confidence in her. None of which was misplaced. Megan had contradictory qualities. Strong feminist ideals but vulnerable and feminine as heck. Playful but serious and responsible. Grounded and optimistic with semi-realistic expectations. Happy to make do with cheap. No desire for extravagance yet understands quality. It will be a while before she stands on her own two feet but if push came to shove, she could survive any storm.

You can go dancing using the moves you know. You can change the order, maybe change things a little but it is the same or pretty much the same. Yes, you may add a new move that has been introduced formally, but this is not what having someone like Megan around is like. We can devise, and scheme, use our imagination. We can jump straight in, no introduction needed. The craft can get more elaborate. She is a touchy-feely person as am I. Thus, the dance enables us to use our bodies to sense one another. Unlike body language, which is there to express happiness, fear, loathing, fright, expectation, and truth. We can use our bodies purely as a tool to tinker, toy, engage, play, stir, communicate, fire up....

I have tried to explain to people what dancing is all about. Most get solo disco trances, bop abouts, arm jangling, rhythm, repetitive ticks, and expression. Most get the idea of two people dancing with one another. What few experience, is something over and above syncopation. It is not better than sex though I have stated that on some occasions. It has an equivalence to it. I have gorged on tantric sex for several hours at a time. Binged on it for years. I would guess that a two-hour dance session is more abundant than two hours of sex. Most have a three-minute hump then roll over and fall asleep. Some extend the activity by edging, getting close to climax, stopping then building back up again. A dance session builds. A bit like getting ever more tipsy the more you drink. Drunk on the engagement with someone special to you.

You know, what brought it all home to me was not the hope of going away together to faraway places but simpler things. I just know she would have accompanied me when I went ice skating. It took me a good twenty minutes to find my feet again. Then I had a thought. We could have made a stab at dancing on ice. We would never win any competitions with me as her partner, but it is the taking part is it not? The last time I had skates on was in Reykjavik. There are rinks aplenty nearby, but the blue lagoon tempts one to make the journey.

Dancing can also be about dressing up for the night. A lot of effort, to add a lot to the occasion. A reasonable spectacle in significant contrast to the gawdy sports clobber that disappoints all bar a few people. "I am wearing my yellow dress tonight", said Megan enthusiastically. Great. Thanks for the heads up after the shops have shut and what an hour before I need to set out. I did manage to colour co-ordinate a few times with her. Good fun. As was the face paint that made her barely recognisable at Halloween. Variety is the spice of life and this spontaneity, this make believe, this distraction, this aspect which marks time, marks an event - makes life so wonderful.

It was sure nice to get back to it. If I go dancing, I will do the talking on the dance floor. It will be much less sitting about from now on. I got around and danced with the majority there. One lady made it excruciating, for she was good. They were all hard to fault in terms of their following, but this one seemed to have been plucked from a nearby nightclub. I probably did a third of the normal number of moves with her. Instead, I tried my best to harmonise. I managed to, to some extent. Close enough. I had a second go with her too. Why not. Excruciating as I am envious as heck, jealous as can be. Someone else has a Megan equivalent. They could do what you can only do with someone you are going out with. Seductive, suave full-on dancing.

Some may dissuade Megan from reading this book. However, I have written the other book. Now let me tell you, it addresses the meaning of life question. It outlines what drives every human being on the planet. And every human being on the planet including compact people, compact dancing people that are known to cut their hair quite short have curiosity hardwired into their DNA. We also care about ourselves the most. Unavoidably so. Thus, ...

If you browse a name directory you might, just might, see the descriptions used to help newly parents select a name for their child.

Laura. Classy, not haughty, a person of substance; prim. Meek at times but has a most excellent ability to belittle, demean and savage you if needed. Can be a lost soul on some occasions but will be the exact opposite in different company.

Megan. Approachable, enthusiastic, endearing with infectious enthusiasm to attempt things. Will give anyone a chance. Only the one chance though.

I had concocted Laura's move and did it with my dear Laura a few times. I had a stack of things lined up to do with Megan. A long list. One entry was of course Megan's move. I won't get to show her so if you happen to meet her maybe you can do it. Place one hand over the other in front of you. Shake your head left to right twice. Swap hands over, shake your head again. Swap them over a second time. Grab her left hand with your right and pull it sharply to the right and glare at her as if she ought to know what an earth that is. She would do this when she started out leading. Is it left over right or right over left? That is no problem, we have all day, but the arm out to the side looking at me like that, is, what the fuck do you want me to do? It neither invites a spin nor a turn, but perplexment. I will miss her because we went through it together. We were both equally useless, equal novices in the opposite lead/follow roles. You can't have that experience again with anyone else.

Megan approached Sarah at the end of an evening and apologised for us using headphones. "It looked like you were having fun, that is the main thing." Sarah knows. And that my dear friends was why we were always so pleased to see one another, that is why we greeted each other so warmly every time. We had fun.

Don't take up Jive.

Three frames made by hand enclose the pictures taken on our dance safari. We took one shot and one shot only at each location. It shall be a reminder of the encounter. I will not dwell on the end. I know what to do now. I have optimism. We made something. We laid down the foundations of max-Jive. I have the badge to prove it. Get yours by completing a few assignments.

Trust actions.

(An injury waiver must be signed beforehand holding only you and your partner responsible for misadventure)

Forward fall

Stand 1.1M apart from your partner. (Adjusted according to height of tallest participant). Fall in together and push apart

with both hands. Both parties must not move their feet.

Balanced lean back.

Stand with all feet level. Both lean back and look skywards. Return partway and release hands for 2 seconds and then return to standing position with feet remaining in start position. Bonus credit given if one party has right leg tucked in between legs of other hooking right foot around right leg of other. (Wrap right leg around left leg of other and in between their legs).

Leading or following blindfolded

One party will be led or asked to lead for 2 minutes competently with eyes closed.

Lead sharing

Jive in a jolly fashion using traditional moves to an art deco song. Perform the lead swap (Laura's move) at the 90 second point.

Lead and lead swap to a routine given on the night

(No prior practice) Routine will be displayed twice and partner consultation time of 3 minutes will be given.

Dance with passion

Demonstrate a good lead and lead swap with a personally preferred genre of style attached to Jive. Maybe Rock or Tango. It must be predominantly lead and follow and contain plenty of well-known and less well-known Jive moves. Please be prepared for early termination if passion is missing. You choose the moves. You choose the song - 5 mins minimum. Discard any belief that the leader is there to make the follower look good.

Performance art

Confidence is required and a clear demonstration of this is expected.

Robot routine. Coin toss for roboteer.

A routine of your own making that proves you have imagination.

Spin

Get dizzy. Some may elect to decline this. A certain allowance will be given for those too world weary. However, one must have shown something extra in other areas.

Link right arm to right arm and turn 30 revolutions in close to 45 seconds.

Hold hands with feet in front of one another. Turn 30 revolutions in close to 45 seconds. Perform two conservation of angular momentum inward pulls.

The badge

In the unlikely event that one or both participants perform to a reasonable standard they will be awarded a bright copper plated badge with selenium infill. The test will be video recorded solely for judging purposes. No explanation or reasons will be given for the inevitable recurrent failure to pass. Badges will be taken off those that are ever found to break the dancing code. Never refuse. Dance with all.

Laura's Move

Lead takes follower's right hand with their right hand. Both step back, left leg lead, right leg follower. Both step inwards and follower is turned anti-clockwise 360 degrees. Followers right arm is placed on leader's left shoulder. Lead places right leg over left leg. Leader holds their head and turns 180 degrees anti-clockwise under follower's arm. Leader places follower's right arm on right shoulder. Both leader and follower steps forward with right leg. The follower may optionally place left arm on leader's left shoulder. Both leader and follower steps back with right leg. Each step forward and back is accompanied by a gradual lowering of the right arms. When arms are at waist height the leader moves to the right. The leader swaps the follower's right hand into the leader's left hand. The leader leads left arm down and to their left to invite a wrap in. The follower turns 360 degrees clockwise and raises left arm to shoulder height at the right side of body. Followers' left palm is raised vertically. Leader connects palms and pushes follower to unwrap anti-clockwise 360 degrees.

The follower becomes the leader, and the ex-leader is now the follower. The move continues in a symmetrical fashion. The leader moves to the right with the follower's right hand kept at waist height. The leader steps back and forth with their right leg raising their right arm. When the arms are at shoulder height the leader crosses their right leg over their left leg. The leader turns anti-clockwise 180 degrees to face the follower. The leader moves arm behind their neck, leans back and has follower's right arm over leader's left shoulder. The leader raises their right arm over their head and turns the follower 360 degrees anti-clockwise.

Megan's Move

Cross arms in front of you, shake head side to side twice. Only Kidding. Lead raises follower's left arm with their right. Leader moves just behind follower staying on their left side, hands rest on follower's shoulder. Both face forward. Leader steps back to straighten arm. In one semi-circular movement pull follower 180 degrees anti-clockwise. Leader pushes arm forward till elbow is on follower's shoulder. Follower places hand on leader's forearm. Leader slides arm back till hand is on shoulder. Leader left leg left one pace. Bend knees and touch right foot next to left foot and bounce right leg back. Bend knees and touch left foot next to right foot and bounce left leg back. Repeat twice. Leader retreat untill right arm is in followers left hand. Swing arm left until elbows close. Offer left hand for follower, repeat with follower now leading same.

They won. I lost. I was defeated. It was victory to Megan's father. Her sister revelled in her influence. All they needed to do was turn us against one another. When Megan went up to her room, they cranked open a bottle of champagne, opening it quietly so that no one heard the cork pop. Cheers. We did it. Not that they would admit it. The empty got stashed at the bottom of the recycling bin. Odd really. Megan's dad could not understand why she would have periods feeling down, feeling low. He sees her buoyant when we were together yet felt the need to burst the bubble.

John took a premium bottle of Prosecco around to Matt's house and they too had a toast. Job well done. They saw two people enjoying themselves. Jo had said she had never seen Megan so happy. Not sure about that as whenever I saw her, she was always quite perky. What she did witness was two that were bold and showcasing the potential of the dance genre. Two that were laughing frequently. Two that came together and danced in unison rather than just together. They saw us outline things that would improve as time went by. Two that revelled in it. The music takes you to a place that ignites feelings, emotions, and joy. We like contrast. A quite afternoon in the open countryside followed by raging noise, melody, and soul. Loud. Real loud. Some looked on at us in disgust. They think it is wrong. An 'old' man with a younger 'girl'. Never mind the result. Racism is heavily condemned, sexism is waning, but ageism is still acceptable. They all use the same mechanism.

Thankfully, good always triumphs over evil, eventually.